Abby's Book

**Other books by
Ann M. Martin**

Leo the Magnificat
Rachel Parker, Kindergarten Show-off
Eleven Kids, One Summer
Ma and Pa Dracula
Yours Turly, Shirley
Ten Kids, No Pets
Slam Book
Just a Summer Romance
Missing Since Monday
With You and Without You
Me and Katie (the Pest)
Stage Fright
Inside Out
Bummer Summer

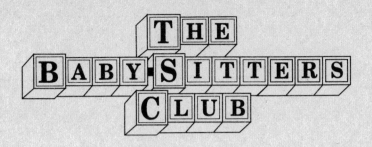

THE BABY-SITTERS CLUB

Abby's Book

Ann M. Martin

AN
APPLE
PAPERBACK

SCHOLASTIC INC.
New York Toronto London Auckland Sydney

No part of this publication may be reproduced in whole or in part, or stored in a retrieval system, or transmitted in any form or by any means, electronic, mechanical, photocopying, recording, or otherwise, without written permission of the publisher. For information regarding permission, write to Scholastic Inc., 555 Broadway, New York, NY 10012.

ISBN 0-590-69182-1

12 11 10 9 8 7 6 5 4 3 2 1   7 8 9/9 0 1 2/0

Printed in the U.S.A.   40

First Scholastic printing, March 1997

The author gratefully acknowledges
Jeanne Betancourt
for her help in
preparing this manuscript.

Abby's Book

CHAPTER 1

The clock radio woke me at 8:00 A.M. "You've heard another fab hour of solid rock and roll," the deejay announced in a booming voice. "Now for a few words from our sponsors. Bellair's Department Store is the one-stop shopping center for the whole family . . ."

Why is it that my clock radio always wakes me with commercials instead of with some of that solid rock and roll?

I turned over, switched off the radio, and lay back, planning the day ahead. It was Saturday. I was coaching softball that morning. Maybe I'd hit the pizza parlor with Kristy at lunch. Then I had soccer practice in the afternoon. I remembered that my mother and my sister and I were having Chinese takeout for dinner and renting a couple of films. What was I forgetting? Oh, yeah. Homework. Well, that could wait until Sunday. My weekend homework probably wouldn't take me more than an hour. Now, what was my weekend homework?

Homework! I bolted straight up, wide awake. I had a huge assignment due on Monday. I had to write a *book*. And I was only planning an hour for homework?! I needed a lifetime. Well, maybe not a lifetime, but I definitely needed more than two days.

I guess you're wondering what the book is about. The book I have to write is about me — Abigail Stevenson. It's an autobiography. Now, I bet you wonder why an eighth-grader is writing an autobiography. Frankly, I don't know. And I don't approve of asking kids to write the story of their own life. We should be living our lives, not writing about them. I also don't approve of long assignments. Maybe, I thought, I should go back to sleep for a little while — like all weekend.

My sister, Anna, knocked on the door and stepped into my room. "Abby, Mom made pancakes. If you want some, you should get up."

"It's Saturday morning." I groaned. "What's the rush?"

"I have orchestra practice at nine and Mom has to work today," Anna answered.

Anna is my twin. We're identical twins, but not the type who do everything the same. I'm a jock. I love sports — especially soccer, softball, and running. I'm also outgoing and always cracking jokes. Anna is quieter than I am — by a lot. She's also a musician, which I am not. Anna can play a load of instruments, including the harmonica and the piano. She's best at the violin, which is her favorite instrument.

People used to mix Anna and me up and call us by each other's names. But not anymore. We don't dress alike — ever. We both have curly black hair but Anna wears her hair short and I wear mine long.

"I didn't know Mom was going to the city today," I told Anna.

"She's meeting one of her writers," Anna explained. "Come on. The pancakes will be cold." Anna went downstairs and I got dressed.

We live in Stoneybrook, Connecticut, but our mother goes to Manhattan every day to work. She's an executive editor at a New York publishing house. You'd think since my mother edits books I wouldn't mind writing one. Forget it.

I walked into the kitchen just as Mom set a plate of blueberry pancakes at my place. I set a pile of papers and photos next to the plate.

"What's all that?" my mother asked.

"Research," I said. "For my autobiography. I thought I'd ask you a few questions during breakfast."

My mother checked her watch. "I'm out of here in five minutes. One of my authors has a big book signing today. I'm taking her to lunch."

"Well, I'm an author too," I said. I pretended to be a news announcer. "Ms. Abigail Stevenson, known for her best-selling autobiography entitled . . ." I hesitated. I needed a title. It came to me like a spark of genius. " . . . entitled *Me, Myself, and I*." I flashed a newscaster's toothy smile at my audience. "It's a touching book, a funny book, and best of all a short book."

My audience of two laughed. But not for long.

"Seriously, Abby," my mother said, "how's the autobiography coming along? It's due on Monday, isn't it?"

I pointed a forkful of pancake at my notes. "I have lots of ideas," I said. "I just have to pull them together, add a few pics, and *whammo!* My masterpiece is done."

My mother turned to Anna. "You turned yours in last week."

"Only because it was due a week earlier than Abby's," Anna explained.

Every eighth-grader at Stoneybrook had to write an autobiography. Which was a good enough reason for me to wish that we'd moved from Long Island to Stoneybrook when I was in ninth grade instead of eighth.

I flipped through my notes and asked Mom questions about my childhood while we ate. I was still asking her questions as she climbed into our minivan to drive to the train station.

After my mother drove away, I stood in the driveway thinking about the interesting fact she'd just told me. Though Anna is older than me by eight minutes, I took my first steps a few hours before she took hers. I wondered if that was why I became more athletic than Anna. Or did I walk independently first because I already was more athletically inclined?

Kristy Thomas came running up to me from the sidewalk. "Hi," she said. "You ready? We'll be late for practice. Get your glove. We better book it."

"Book it?" I said. "I'm booking it, all right." I held up the notebook I'd been using for my interview with my mother. "Autobiography. All weekend. I am seriously bummed."

"Too bad," said Kristy. She gave me a little punch on the arm. "Good luck." She went off.

"Thanks," I yelled. Of all my new friends, Kristy's the one who's most like me.

We're both outgoing and smart. (Even though I don't like homework — or writing books — I *am* pretty smart.) And we both love sports. Kristy coaches a softball team for little kids called Kristy's Krushers. I'm her assistant coach.

There are ways Kristy and I are different too. Kristy is more organized than I am and much bossier. However, her bossiness can be a plus. You see, Kristy is the president and brains behind this great club I belong to, the Babysitters Club (or BSC).

Here's another way Kristy and I are different. She comes from a huge blended family. In my family it's just Anna, my mom, and me. Our dad died in a car accident when Anna and I were nine. I still miss him and think of him every single day. Kristy lost her dad too. Only in Kristy's case, her father ran away.

I'm not the only BSC member who's experienced the death of a parent. Mary Anne Spier's mother died when Mary Anne was an infant. After Mary Anne's mother died, her family was even smaller than mine — there was only her and her dad. That changed when Mr. Spier married his high school sweetheart and they brought their two families together. Now Mary Anne has a stepmother, a stepbrother, and a terrific stepsister, Dawn Schafer, who is an honorary member of the BSC. Right now, Dawn is living in California with her father and brother. But she comes to visit, so I've met her. I can see why Mary Anne and the other members of the club miss Dawn. She's really cool.

Mary Anne is the secretary of the BSC. She keeps track of our baby-sitting jobs in the club record book and makes sure that we all write in the club notebook. Mary Anne is the perfect person for that job because she is super-neat and super-conscientious.

Our treasurer is Stacey McGill. Stacey loves math and is excellent at it. That girl knows just where to put a decimal point. She also knows how to dress.

Stacey and I have something major in common. We both suffer from annoying, chronic illnesses. (A chronic illness is one that doesn't go away.) Stacey's chronic illness is diabetes. She can't eat desserts or sweets. She has to check her blood and give herself insulin injections every day.

I have allergies and asthma. I'm allergic to lots of foods, such as milk products and shellfish. I'm also allergic to most stuff that floats through the air — dog hair, dust, and pollen. The allergies and asthma are connected. They both affect my ability to breathe, especially the asthma. I use an inhaler when I feel an asthma attack coming on, but I still land in the hospital a couple of times a year. Not being able to breathe is pretty scary.

I don't make a big deal about my illnesses. (Neither does Stacey.) I refuse to let it get me down or to keep me from doing the things I love, such as sports. I think I'll outgrow some of my allergies and hope the asthma might just disappear too.

The vice president of the BSC is Claudia Kishi. Claudia is really cool. I love her kooky way of dressing. Yesterday, for example, she wore leopard-skin tights with a black velvet minidress to school. Her earrings were made out of fake-fur buttons. (She made them herself.) Claudia is what you'd call a theme dresser, and yesterday the theme was "jungle."

We have our club meetings three times a week (Mondays, Wednesdays, and Fridays) in Claudia's room, which is equipped with a private phone line — perfect for our BSC calls — and an inexhaustible supply of junk food for our personal pleasure.

The BSC has two other regular members, Mallory Pike and Jessi Ramsey. They are both sixth-graders and junior officers of the club. Mal and Jessi are best friends.

Mal loves literature and wants to write and

illustrate children's books. She can't wait to be an eighth-grader and write her autobiography. It'll be a snap for Mal.

Jessi is a fabulous ballet dancer. She studies ballet as seriously as my sister studies the violin, which is *very* seriously!

The BSC also has two associate members, Logan Bruno and Shannon Kilbourne. Associate members fill in when the BSC has more jobs than the regular members can handle. Logan and Shannon don't have to come to the meetings all the time like the rest of us. By the way, Logan is Mary Anne's boyfriend, and Shannon and my sister are close friends.

So that's the BSC and my new group of friends. I still miss my friends from Long Island, where I lived before moving here. Except for having to write the story of my life, I love living in Stoneybrook, Connecticut.

Anna appeared beside me on the driveway. "Penny for your thoughts," she said.

"I'll tell you for a buck fifty," I said with a grin.

"I'm saving my money to buy your book," she quipped.

"I guess I have to write it if I'm going to make the best-seller list."

"I guess you have to write it if you're going

to pass English," Anna pointed out.

Anna went to orchestra practice and I went to my room. It was time to work on my autobiography. It was a story that no one could write but *me, myself, and I.*

me, myself, and I :
The Autobiography of
Abigail Stevenson

From Birth to Backpack

CHAPTER 2

My mom and dad knew that they were having twins. They even knew that we'd be identical girls. What they didn't know was that we would arrive a month earlier than scheduled.

Dad was on a business trip and Mom was home alone. They'd just moved to a two-bedroom apartment in a new neighborhood and hadn't unpacked their stuff yet.

"I was so big with the two of you," my mother told me, "that I couldn't even think of unpacking those boxes. Since you weren't due for a month, your father and I thought there would be plenty of time for him to settle us in the new place when he came back from his trip. So there I sat on October fifteenth — big as a house in the middle of this mess — trying to imagine what it would be like to have identical baby girls. That's when I realized you were going to be born a lot sooner than we thought."

Mom phoned our dad at his environmental engineering meeting in Chicago. He left the meeting immediately to catch the first flight back to New York. Next, Mom called her doctor and described how she felt. The doctor told her to have someone drive her to the hospital right away. Since Mom didn't know any of her neighbors yet, she called a car service.

The guy who drove her was pretty nervous. "You think you're going to have that baby in the car, ma'am?" he asked.

"Babies," Mom said, correcting him. "I'm having twins." The poor man almost drove onto the lawn when he heard that!

Mom didn't have us in the car, though. And our dad walked into the delivery room just as Anna was being born.

Eight minutes later I popped into the world.

"Some people don't think newborns are cute," my father used to say. "But you girls were beautiful from the get-go."

Rachel and Jonathan Stevenson
have been doubly blessed
Anna Stevenson
and
Abigail Stevenson
born October 15th

Double the trouble,
double the fun!

15

Mom says that when she came home from the hospital with Anna and me, the whole apartment was set up. Dad had unpacked everything and put it away. And the nursery was perfectly furnished and decorated. Dad had bought and put up the balloon-patterned curtains Mom had admired in the store, but that they'd put off buying. He had also hung two fish mobiles over our new cribs.

"On top of everything else he did," she said, "he surprised me with a rocking chair for your room."

That's the kind of man my dad was. Thoughtful and generous.

I asked Mom if it was hard to raise two babies at the same time. "It was difficult," she said. "But after a few months, you entertained one another. If one of you was fussing, I'd put her in the crib with the other one, and the fussy baby would quiet down. That was a big help."

One of my first memories is of thinking I was looking at Anna when I was actually seeing myself in the mirror. It took me a long time to tell the difference between my sister and my own reflection.

Another early memory I have is being with my dad and Anna at a playground. Anna and I were playing on the slide. Dad was standing at the bottom to catch us. I'd just slid down and was waiting with him at the bottom of the slide for Anna. Suddenly a bully at the top of the slide pushed past Anna and she tumbled to the ground.

Dad ran to her. I crumbled where I stood and started crying. I thought I'd been hurt too. Dad had two crying kids to deal with. One *really* hurt (Anna sprained her ankle) and the other one *thinking* she was hurt.

He had to carry both of us home. I remember my ankle truly hurting, and I insisted on having an Ace bandage just like Anna's.

Because Anna and I mostly played at home with one another, we didn't know for the first few years of our lives that being an identical twin was unusual.

When we were three years old, Mom and Dad decided that we should learn to play with other kids. So, after our third birthday, they enrolled us in a pre-school.

While Anna was meeting the teacher, I checked out the playroom for twins. But I couldn't find any pairs of identical kids other than Anna and me.

My mother called to me. I was in the block corner. I could see her over the top of the block pile, but my sister was blocked (get it?) from my view. I panicked. Was this a place where

My dad could always
make me laugh.

half of you — your twin — disappeared?

I started screaming, and my mother and Anna came running to me. Because I was crying, Anna started crying too. Only Anna and I understood what had upset me. And at that age we weren't very good at explaining things to other people.

You see, Anna and I had developed our own private language for communicating between ourselves. Because we understood one another so well, we didn't bother to learn to speak English as quickly as most kids do. I've heard this happens a lot with twins. I can't remember any of the words of our secret language now. Neither can Anna.

It was because of our language that our parents decided to send us to pre-school. And sure enough, it worked. There were lots of interesting things to do there, and plenty of kids we wanted to talk to. We learned to speak English very quickly.

Our teacher, Ms. Randolph, loved having identical twins in her class. "You girls are so *cute*," she used to say. She didn't even mind that she could barely tell us apart.

Even though we dressed alike, Anna and I were already interested in different activities. Anna liked musical instruments and I always begged to play outdoors on the jungle gym.

By the end of each day, Ms. Randolph had an easier time telling us apart. I was the dirty twin and Anna was the one in the corner playing with the plastic guitar.

Here's one of the things I didn't like about being twins. People stare at you. Even now, when Anna and I dress differently and have different hair styles, strangers often stare when they see the two of us together. They'll say something brilliant like, "You two are twins, aren't you?"

When we were very little, perfect strangers would talk to us. They'd say we were adorable and ask our parents, "However do you tell them apart?"

Most of the time Anna and I hated it when someone made a big deal out of our twin-ness. Anna would duck her head and not look at the person. But I'd stare right back. Sometimes I'd make a silly face. If the person said "And what's *your* name?" I'd answer for both of us.

Sometimes I'd reverse us and say, "I'm Anna and she's Abby." My dad would wink at me to let me know that he knew who was who. After the person left, we'd laugh about our joke.

One day, when we were five years old, we were at the mall with our mother when we noticed another set of identically dressed twins walking across the center court, carrying identical shopping bags. They were women about the age of our grandmothers. When the twins spotted us, they hurried over to us.

"Well, well," one of them said.

"Look at these girls," said the other. Their voices and expressions were identical too.

"I'm Jan Sanders," said one.

"I'm Jean Sanders," said the other.

My mother introduced us. Even though I wasn't usually shy, for some reason I felt shy in front of the Sanders twins.

"Do you always dress alike?" my mother asked them.

"My, yes," answered both twins with a laugh.

They held up their identical shopping bags. "Sweaters," said Jan.

"We live in identical houses next door to one another," said Jean. Or was it Jan? I'd already lost track of which was which.

"The only thing that isn't identical is . . ." began one.

" . . . our husbands," finished the other. They giggled.

Then they squatted so they could look Anna and me in the eyes.

"It's wonderful to have an identical twin," said one.

"You always have your best, best friend close by," said the other.

"Always looking alike."

"Always thinking alike."

"Doing the same things."

"Always together," they said in unison.

Jean and Jan looked lovingly at one another and smiled. "Two peas in a pod."

I noticed that people walking past us were staring. I heard someone say, "Wow. Two sets of twins. I wonder if they're related?"

That afternoon, Anna and I had an argument about what game to play. I wanted to play with a ball in the backyard and she wanted to color in our new coloring books. In the end, we did a little of both. I wondered if Jean and Jan ever argued.

Even though Anna and I disagreed from time to time, I knew that we argued far less than our friends did with their brothers and sisters. For instance, we had no trouble sharing toys.

We had identical doctor's kits, identical baby dolls, identical collections of stuffed animals, and the same make-your-own-necklace kits. Those were all gifts. But even when we picked out our own toys, we usually wanted the same thing. It made life pretty simple and balanced for us and our parents.

Until my dad took us to pick out school supplies for first grade.

The school had sent a list:

From the desk of Mrs. Rothchild

First graders are to arrive for the
first day of school with the
following supplies:
  1 backpack
  1 three-ring binder with dividers
  1 pencil case
  4 sharpened pencils
  1 gummy eraser
  1 pair blunt plastic scissors
  1 box crayola crayons
  (no more than 24 colors, please)

Louise Rothchild

Anna and I were very excited. We'd seen big kids walking to the elementary school wearing backpacks. Now *we* were the big kids.

There was a store at the mall with three long rows of school supplies. It was buzzing with kids picking out their stuff for the first day of school. We started out in the backpack aisle.

Anna and I stared at the five rows of hanging backpacks. They came in a rainbow of colors and a lot of them were covered with pictures and words. I noticed a *Sesame Street* backpack (too young), a Spiderman backpack (not my style), a Barbie doll one (too pink for my taste), a backpack in the shape of a teddy bear (too silly).

Anna agreed with me in rejecting all of the above. So when she yelled out, "There it is. There's my backpack," I assumed it was the same one I had just spotted in the top row.

My choice was a green pack covered with sports symbols. I could see a baseball, a basketball, and a pair of ice skates imprinted on it. I couldn't wait for Dad to take it down so I could see what else was on my new backpack.

But Anna wasn't pointing at the sports backpack. She was pointing to the bottom rack at a backpack shaped like a grand piano. It had a pattern of white and black keys running up the side. When Anna and I realized that we'd chosen different backpacks, we just stared at one another.

can you tell which one is me?

Dad sized up the situation very quickly. "Okay," he said. "Anna gets the piano. Abby, you can have the sports pack."

I felt very weird inside. We almost always had the same things. I couldn't imagine going to first grade looking different from Anna. "No," I said. "I don't want it."

"Do you want the piano like Anna?" he asked.

I shook my head no. I couldn't explain why, but I felt horribly sad.

Then Anna started to cry, which made me cry too. "I don't want the piano anymore," she sobbed. "I don't want a backpack. I don't want to go to first grade."

"Me neither," I said.

Dad comforted us. And in the end, we picked out identical school supplies. Plain purple backpacks and notebooks with a rainbow design.

When we walked into first grade two days later, no one but our parents could tell us apart.

Red and Blue Just Won't Do

CHAPTER 3

Anna and I stood hand in hand in front of our first grade teacher, Mrs. Rothchild. She looked from one of us to the other. "Identical twins," she said with a wince. That was the first and only time I remember anyone being disappointed that there were two of us. Mrs. Rothchild quickly transformed her wince into a teacher-smile and showed us where to sit. Anna went to the first seat, first row, and I was sent to the fourth seat, last row.

Elvia, a red-haired girl I recognized from kindergarten, was assigned to the seat next to mine. "Which one are you?" she asked.

"Abby," I answered.

"What's the other one's name?" she asked.

"Anna," I answered.

"Oh, yeah," Elvia grinned. "Anna and Abby."

A girl I didn't know sat in the seat next to me.

"Rema!" Elvia exclaimed. "Yeah! You're in our class." Pointing to me, Elvia told Rema, "This is Anna. Her sister's name is Abby. They're twins. They look exactly alike."

"I'm Abby," I told Elvia.

Elvia shrugged her shoulders. "I told you I can't tell."

"Hi, Abby-Anna," said Rema.

"Hey, neat," laughed Elvia. "*Abby-Anna.* I'll call both of you 'Abby-Anna.' Then I won't make a mistake."

I slumped in my seat. So far, I didn't like first grade.

By the end of the first week, all of the kids in the class were calling us Abby-Anna.

"It's weird," said Anna.

"I hate it," I said.

As our class was leaving the room on Friday

afternoon, Mrs. Rothchild called, "Anna, could you come here, please?" Anna was already out the door, so I knew Mrs. Rothchild was talking to me. I didn't bother to tell her I was Abby, not Anna. At least she wasn't calling me "Abby-Anna."

Mrs. Rothchild handed me a sealed envelope. "Please give this note to your parents."

Mom had just started a publishing job in New York City and didn't arrive home until six-thirty or later. But Dad had fixed his schedule at work so he could pick us up after school every day. Anna and I loved being with Dad during those hours between the end of school and when Mom came home.

Sometimes Dad had office work to do at home, but we knew we could interrupt him anytime. He'd almost always take time out to play ball with us or listen to music and play board games. Then we'd keep him company while he made dinner. Sometimes we helped with the cooking and we always set the table.

The day Mrs. Rothchild gave me the note, Dad was waiting for us outside school as usual. I handed him the sealed envelope. "It's for you," I explained. "From our teacher."

"You two already in trouble?" Dad asked with a grin.

Anna shook her head and mumbled, "I don't think so."

"Nah," I said. "We're not in trouble. But Mrs. Rothchild doesn't like that we're twins. I can tell."

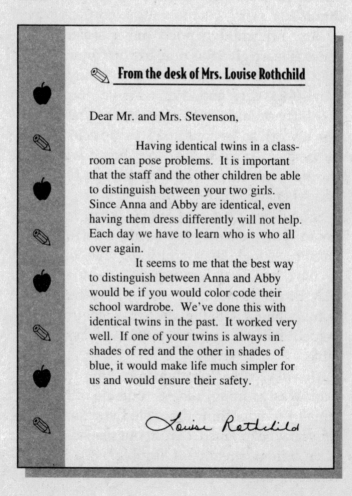

✎ **From the desk of Mrs. Louise Rothchild**

Dear Mr. and Mrs. Stevenson,

     Having identical twins in a class-room can pose problems. It is important that the staff and the other children be able to distinguish between your two girls. Since Anna and Abby are identical, even having them dress differently will not help. Each day we have to learn who is who all over again.

     It seems to me that the best way to distinguish between Anna and Abby would be if you would color code their school wardrobe. We've done this with identical twins in the past. It worked very well. If one of your twins is always in shades of red and the other in shades of blue, it would make life much simpler for us and would ensure their safety.

Louise Rothchild

At home, Dad put out a snack of juice and cookies. When the three of us were sitting around the table, he finally opened the note from our teacher and read it out loud.

Mrs. Rothchild's letter went on to explain that if Anna or I were in a dangerous situation — such as walking under a falling brick — she wanted to know which name to call out in warning. I thought that was pretty dumb, but Dad said she had a point.

"But Dad, our school isn't made of bricks," I argued.

"It could be anything falling," Dad explained, "like a flowerpot or a notebook. Or what if a swerving car was about to hit you?"

"I promise I'll look up when anyone shouts 'Anna,'" I said. "Besides, I don't even like blue."

"I like blue," said Anna.

"Then it's settled," said Dad. "Anna wears blue and Abby wears red."

When Mom came home, my father showed her the letter. She agreed with Dad that we should try color coding for school. So after dinner, we went to Anna's and my bedroom and put all the red clothing from our wardrobe into my drawers and all the blue clothing into Anna's drawers.

"You can wear your yellow, purple, and

green clothes on weekends," my father joked.

I ended up with two red T-shirts, two pink blouses, matching red sweaters, a bunch of red socks, two identical red wool skirts, and two red baseball caps.

Anna had all my blue clothes, except my blue jeans. Mom said I could wear those as long as I wore a red top with them.

On Monday morning Anna and I went to school dressed in our colors. Mrs. Rothchild was all smiles. "Well, that's better," she said. "Red for Anna and blue for Abby."

"It's the other way around," I told her. "I'm Abby."

"Right," she said with a frown. "Well, go to your places."

I didn't like this color coding business. Especially when Mrs. Rothchild explained it to the other kids in the class. For some reason they thought it was hilarious. Even when Mrs. Rothchild explained the falling brick idea, there were a few giggles.

For the rest of the day, Mrs. Rothchild had no trouble keeping Anna and me straight, but the kids didn't bother to separate us by color. They'd already decided we were both Abby-Anna.

"Abby-Anna, wanna play kickball during recess?" Elvia asked, even though I was sitting at the desk right next to her so she knew that I was Abby.

I thought I hated the Abby-Anna name more than anything, but by the end of the day, we had nicknames I hated even more.

During indoor recess that afternoon, Rema and I were standing with Anna next to Anna's desk. Todd, this kid who sat behind Anna, stepped up to us. "Hey, Blue," he said to Anna, "got a pencil I can borrow?"

Anna handed him a pencil. But her face was turning beet red with embarrassment and anger. She hated being called by her color.

A few other boys heard Todd call Anna "Blue" and cracked up. One of them said, "Blue is for boys and pink is for girls." He pointed to Anna. "Maybe this one is a boy."

Well, that cracked up the boys even more, and I wanted to crack their heads open.

I punched Todd on the arm. "Her name is *Anna*," I shouted.

Mrs. Rothchild clapped her hands to signal the end of recess.

"Abby, take your seat," ordered Mrs. Rothchild. "Boys, calm down."

There were a bunch of kids in our class who

loved to tease. After that, Anna and I were Blue or Red to most of the boys. The rest of the kids — the girls and our friends — called us Abby-Anna. There was a two-week period when the only people who called us by our proper names were Mrs. Rothchild and our parents.

I couldn't wait for weekends, when we could dress alike in whatever colors we wanted and be called by our own names.

On Saturday morning, Anna and I dressed identically in white T-shirts with green cardigan sweaters and black jeans. Mom had gone to work in the city that day, so it was just the three of us for breakfast. Dad was cooking up our favorite (his, too) — walnut waffles with maple syrup.

"So how's this color thing working out at school?" he asked when we were gobbling down seconds.

"Awful!" I said.

"You mean they still can't keep you straight?" he asked.

"That part is okay," I answered.

"Well, then," he said, "what's the problem?"

I could feel that Anna didn't want me to tell our father that the kids were teasing us with our color names. Anna and I had an unspoken arrangement that we had to agree about something before we told our parents. So I didn't tell Dad how much we hated the color coding and that being an identical twin had become a major pain for both of us.

CHAPTER 4

After breakfast, we went back to our room to talk privately. I asked Anna why she wouldn't tell Dad that we didn't like the color coding.

"I don't want to make Daddy unhappy," she explained.

"But he's our father," I said. "We should tell him."

Anna shook her head.

I understood how Anna felt, but I also wanted to fix what was going wrong for us at school. I tried to convince Anna.

"We're not totally, positively alike," I told her. "I don't want to be like those twins in the shopping mall."

"Me neither," agreed Anna.

"But everybody at school thinks we're like that," I said.

"They know we're different."

"No, they don't. Only Mom and Dad can tell us apart."

"Mrs. Rothchild can," said Anna.

"Mrs. Rothchild doesn't think *we're* different," I told Anna. "All she knows is that red and blue are different."

"Our friends can tell us apart."

"Who? They call us both Abby-Anna."

"They just like to kid around," said Anna. "It's a game."

I still hadn't convinced my sister that we were seen as copies of the same person and that we had to do something about it.

Finally, I came up with a brilliant idea that would prove to Anna that people really couldn't tell us apart.

"On Monday, let's switch clothes," I told her. "We'll pretend we're each other. I'll be Anna and you be Abby. Then you'll see. No one will know the difference, even Mrs. Rothchild. She'll still call the girl dressed in red, sitting in the fourth row Abby and the girl dressed in blue in the first row Anna."

"I don't know," murmured Anna.

"Come on, Anna," I pleaded. "It'll be *fun*. You'll see. No one will be able to tell."

Finally, before we went to bed on Sunday

night, she agreed. "We'll switch clothes at school," I told her, "so Mom and Dad won't know."

"If we both wear blue jeans," Anna suggested, "we'll only have to change tops."

When we walked into school the next morning, we went straight to the girls' room, ducked into a stall, and exchanged shirts.

When we went into our classroom, Anna automatically headed for her seat in the first row. I gave her a little push toward the other end of the room. "See you at recess, *Abby*," I said.

I sat in Anna's seat in front of Todd. "Hey, Blue," he said, "how about a pencil?"

I turned around and glared at him. "My name is not *Blue*. And bring your own pencils." As soon as I said it, I knew I'd made a mistake. My sister would never talk back to Todd like that.

Todd looked a little surprised. "Forget it, Blue," he growled. "I don't need your old pencil." A minute later, Todd was kicking my chair and chanting under his breath. "Blue, Blue, how do you do?"

I pretended I was Anna and didn't say anything.

After the Pledge of Allegiance, Mrs. Rothchild always announced the name of the student who would sing the first line of "My Country 'Tis of Thee." It was a different student every day, and I had had my turn the week before. I hated doing it. I didn't have a good voice. The morning that I was Anna, Mrs. Rothchild said, "Anna, today you will begin the song."

Everyone waited for Anna to begin. Why wasn't she singing? I wondered. I turned around to see what was going on with Anna and realized that everyone was looking at me. Oops. *I* was Anna, so I had to sing the first line of "My Country 'Tis of Thee" again.

So far, I didn't like being Anna.

Later Anna and I walked out to the playground together. "*Abby*," I said, "what will we do for recess?"

"I don't know, *Anna*," my sister said to me.

Elvia and Rema ran to us. "Come play kickball, Abby-Anna," said Rema.

"I'm going to the library to get another book," Anna told our friends.

"*Abby*, you love kickball," I said. I jabbed her waist with my elbow as a reminder.

Anna looked a little confused for a second, then jumped around shouting, "Yes. I love kickball. Let's play kickball!"

I had to laugh. She was imitating me and it wasn't like her at all. How could anyone think that Anna and I were just copies of the same person?

As we were walking back to our classroom after recess, Anna whispered in my ear, "I want to switch back. I don't want to be you anymore."

Just then I saw the last person in the world I expected to see at school that day. Dad! I wanted to hide. Would he be mad that we'd switched places? Would he tell our teacher? Would we get into big trouble?

My father put an arm around each of us.

"Dad," I said, "what are you doing here?"

"I have to go to the Pine Barrens this afternoon. Mrs. Trono from next door will pick you up after school and stay with you until I get home. I came to tell you."

"Oh, okay," I said. Anna didn't say anything. She was too frightened that Dad would know we were playing a trick on our teacher and classmates.

"I'll see you around five," said Dad. "Meanwhile, behave yourselves."

"You too," I said in the joking way I had with him. Then I thought, I'm Anna today and Anna would never joke like that. I should act like Anna, even in front of Dad. And then I thought, Dad must already know that we've switched. He can tell us apart no matter what.

Just then, Dad bent over and kissed me on the forehead. " 'Bye, Anna," he said.

I watched in amazement as he kissed Anna on the head and said, " 'Bye, Abby."

As Dad walked away, Elvia said, "Boy, Abby-Anna, you have a great dad. He's so nice."

He might be nice, I thought, but he doesn't even know his own daughters. I felt like someone had just punched me in the chest, and it took me a second to get my breath back.

During the rest of the day I didn't even try to pretend I was Anna. But still, no one seemed to notice that I was taking my sister's place.

As we were leaving the classroom that afternoon, Mrs. Rothchild stopped us. Maybe she at least had noticed that Anna and I had switched places. A smile spread across her face. "Girls," she said, "I want to thank you for being so cooperative about wearing separate colors. It really does help the rest of us. I'm sure you must get bored wearing the same color all the time, but you'll get used to it."

As we walked away, I thought unhappily about the rest of my life at school. I would never be Abby. I'd always be the red one. And Anna, who'd never be known for her real self, would always be the blue one.

Mrs. Trono met us outside school. "Well, you two look sad enough to make me weep," she said with a wink. "What's up?"

"Nothing," Anna and I said in unison.

I didn't joke around with Mrs. Trono the way I usually did. Why bother being myself and being different from Anna if no one knew we were different? After all, even our own father couldn't tell us apart.

CHAPTER 5

Dad came home an hour or so after we did. He was carrying a big bag of groceries and acting like his jolly self. But Anna and I felt terrible. We were still upset that Dad couldn't tell us apart.

"Hey, hey," Dad said, "spaghetti and meatballs tonight. You girls can make the meatballs. Nice big ones."

I didn't roll my eyes and say, "I *love* meatballs," like I usually did.

As soon as Mrs. Trono left, Dad whispered to us, "How did the switch at school work out? Did you two trick Mrs. Rothchild too?"

I couldn't believe my ears. Dad hadn't mixed me up with Anna after all!

"Were you joking when you called us by each other's names?" Anna asked.

"Of course I was joking," Dad said. "I figured if you were switching you had a reason and you'd tell me all about it tonight."

Tears welled up in my eyes. "I was scared," I told him. "I didn't think you knew me."

"Me too," said Anna. She began to cry.

Tears suddenly appeared in Dad's eyes too. He wrapped both of us in a big bear hug. "You two," he said. "I could tell you apart from the moment I first held you." He kissed Anna on her forehead. "You're my Anna," he said. Then he kissed me. A soft, sweet kiss. "And you are my Abby." He laughed. "And I would bet my life that the switch was Abby's idea."

"It was," I said. And I hugged him with all my might.

While we helped make dinner, Anna and I told Dad the whole story. Dad asked us how it felt to be in Mrs. Rothchild's class.

"Everybody acts like we're the same person," I said.

"Even though you wear different colors?" asked Dad.

Anna and I nodded.

"I don't want to wear red anymore," I said. "It's stupid."

"It's no fun," agreed Anna.

"I want to wear any colors that I want to school," I said. "Even blue!"

My dad stopped stirring the sauce and

watched us making meatballs for a couple of seconds. "Well, there is one thing you could do that would make you look really different from one another."

"What?" we asked in unison.

"It has something to do with your gorgeous long hair," he said.

I clutched my curls. "Cut our hair?!" I exclaimed.

"Just one of you," he said. "If one of you had short hair and one had long, it would be very easy for people to tell you apart, no matter what you wore."

"I won't cut my hair!" I said.

"Me neither," said Anna.

"Maybe you don't want to be different after all," Dad commented.

"We *do*," Anna and I told him.

"Think about it, then," he said.

By the time our mother came home, Anna and I had done a lot of thinking. We knew it was a good idea. But neither of us wanted to be the one with short hair.

During dinner, we told Mom about the switch. Like Dad, Mom asked us lots of questions about how we felt when people treated us like the same person.

"Your father has a good idea," Mom said. "If one of you cuts your hair, it would help. But the one who has the short haircut shouldn't do it unless she really wants shorter hair."

After dinner, Anna and I went to our room. "I still don't want to cut my hair," I said.

Anna didn't say anything. She went to the mirror and held her hair up so that it looked short. I stood next to her. We *would* look different if one of us had short hair. "You look pretty," I said. And I meant it.

Anna smiled at her reflection. "I like it," she said.

We ran downstairs to tell our parents the news.

The next day was a holiday from school, and Dad didn't have to go to work, either. After Mom left for her job in New York City, the three of us ate breakfast at the mall and then went to Hair Today. A beautician named Missy said she could take us right away.

Anna sat in the big chair. I could feel how nervous she was.

"It's going to look so cool," I said encouragingly.

"You two have beautiful hair," Missy said, "but life will be a lot easier with short hair."

"I know," said Anna with a smile.

I felt a twinge when Missy took the first cut of Anna's hair. A long curl fell to the floor. As Missy snipped her way around Anna's head, I

48

held onto the bottom of my own hair, just to be sure that my curls weren't falling to the floor with Anna's. Anna kept her eyes on herself in the mirror. The more Missy cut, the happier Anna was.

Finally, Missy stepped back and grinned at Anna's reflection. "Done!" she proudly exclaimed.

As Anna stepped down from the chair, Missy made a little bow to me. "Next," she said.

"Not me!" I shouted. "I'm not having my hair cut!"

As we walked out of the beauty parlor, I saw our reflection in the mirror. We did look different! I would never again be confused with my sister. And Anna and I would never be like Jean and Jan Sanders — the identical twins we met at the shopping mall.

"Let's get you two some new clothes while we're here," said Dad. "And instead of buying two of everything, how would you like to pick out separate outfits?"

Anna and I checked with one another and then told Dad yes.

My dad always had the best ideas.

I picked out blue jean overalls and a light-yellow shirt. Anna picked out a flower-print dress. We'd outgrown our jean jackets, so I wanted a new one. But Anna wanted a fleece pullover instead of a jean jacket. We each got what we wanted. I couldn't wait for school the next day.

When we entered the classroom, Rema and Elvia ran to Anna. "Abby-Anna," she said. "You got your hair cut. It looks so great."

"I love it!" exclaimed Elvia.

"You look like you're in *third* grade," added Rema.

For a second, I wished I were the one who had the haircut.

Finally, Rema and Elvia noticed me. "You didn't get your hair cut? How come?" Elvia asked.

"So we'd look different," I said. "And everyone could *really* tell us apart."

"And not call us Abby-Anna," added Anna.

Mrs. Rothchild approached us. She looked happy. "Tell me which one is Abby and which one is Anna," she said. "You'll only have to tell me once."

I laughed. "I'm Abby."

"Good," she said.

With our new, separate looks, the kids in the class started treating us like separate people.

Anna became best friends with Lydia, who took private music lessons. Soon Anna was taking music lessons too. But I didn't want to take music. I wanted to be a Brownie. So when Anna was at her music class, I went to Brownie meetings with Rema and Elvia.

October fifteenth was our birthday. It was a Saturday, so our birthday party was on the very day of our birthday. We invited all the girls from our first grade class to the party. Dad and Mom stayed up late the night before making a special surprise cake. I was so excited I could hardly sleep.

Finally, it was time for our birthday party. Dad organized games for us to play in the backyard. After that, it was time for cake and presents. I couldn't wait.

The first surprise was the cake — or should I say cakes? Instead of one cake for both of us and one singing of "Happy Birthday," we each had our own small cake and our own song.

"First, Anna's cake," Mom said. "Because she was born first."

Everyone, including me, sang "Happy Birthday" to Anna. Her cake was shaped like a grand piano, just like the backpack she had wanted for school.

Then it was my turn. Everyone sang to me as my mother and father presented me with my cake. It was round and decorated like a kickball. I loved having my own cake.

my very own birthday cake!

Then the presents. Anna opened one, then I opened one.

Elvia gave me a game of jacks and some stickers. She gave Anna a tape of classical music for her Walkman. Almost everyone gave us different presents. It was the first time in our lives that people didn't give us identical gifts.

Anna and I now agree that our sixth birthday party was the best ever. We both felt special in our own way.

Without Dad

CHAPTER 6

I was a very happy kid when I started fourth grade. Being a twin wasn't a problem at school anymore. Anna and I were in different classes, we each had our own set of friends, and I was going to "fly up" from Brownies to Girl Scouts. So I thought that fourth grade was going to be the best year yet.

But in November — in a split second — something happened that changed my life forever.

It was a sunny morning and I came bouncing down the stairs ready for another happy day. I was wearing jeans, a turtleneck, and a cowboy vest my grandmother had given me for my ninth birthday. Anna walked down the stairs behind me. She liked to wear skirts to school and definitely moved at a slower pace than I did.

When I came into the kitchen, Dad was setting the table for breakfast and Mom was rushing out the door. " 'Bye, guys," she said. "See you tonight." She checked her watch. If Mom missed her train, she'd be late for work. "Jonathan, don't forget to give Anna a check for her violin teacher," she said.

Dad blew her a kiss, but she was already gone.

Dad saw me notice that Mom didn't see him blow her the kiss. He patted me on the head. "That kiss will catch her," he said. "My kisses always do." We all laughed at that.

Dad rubbed his hands together gleefully. "So, young ladies, what'll it be this morning? Cereal with bananas or bananas with cereal?"

"Cereal with bananas," said Anna.

"I'll have lactose-free milk," I said, "with a side of cereal and bananas."

Every weekday during breakfast, Anna and

I reminded Dad what we each had to do after school. "I have my violin lesson today," Anna said.

"I'll pick you up after school and drive you over to Randal's house," he said. "Then I'll shop for groceries and come back and pick you up."

"Don't forget to give her a check for Randal," I reminded Dad. We all kidded Dad about his absent-mindedness.

"Check on the check," he said with a grin. "Are you with me for all the above, Abby? Or do you have plans of your own?"

"Elvia invited me to her house to play soccer with the kids on her block. Okay?"

"Sure," he said. "I'll pick you up after Anna's violin lesson. Elvia lives close to the school, so I guess you guys will walk there."

I nodded.

"Be careful crossing the street," he said. "There're some crazy drivers out there."

"Da-ad," I said. "I know how to cross the street. I'm nine years old."

"Aa-by," he said, mimicking me. "Ex-cu-use me." He was so funny when he talked like that, you had to laugh.

Dad walked us to the bus stop, like always. I remember every second of that walk — what we all said and how I felt. I especially remember my dad's parting words. The school bus was coming toward us. "How about spaghetti and meatballs tonight?" he said.

"Great," I said. The doors on the school bus opened for us. Before I followed Anna up the steps, I turned to tell Dad, "I *love* meatballs." I rolled my eyes at him like I always did when we talked about meatballs.

I waved to Dad out the window when the bus passed him.

He blew me a kiss.

A few hours later, I was walking back from the lunchroom with Elvia. "I can't wait to play soccer," I told Elvia. I kicked a make-believe ball along the hall. "I could play all day."

"Me too," said Elvia.

Our teacher, Mr. Kiefer, met us at the classroom door. I noticed he looked very upset, and I wondered why.

"Abby," he said. "I need you to come to the principal's office with me." The way he said it gave me chills. I knew something was wrong. I was afraid to ask him what it was. So we walked silently down the hall. I wasn't worried that *I'd* done something wrong. I was just scared.

Grandpa Morris — my mother's father — was in the principal's office waiting for me.

What was Grandpa Morris doing here? I wondered. For an instant I thought he'd come to see us at school as a surprise. But I couldn't hold onto that idea because I could see tears in his eyes. Then I noticed that Anna was walking into the office behind me.

"Abby," he said in a choked voice. "Anna." He moved toward us. I took a step away from my own grandfather. I felt afraid of him. I had never seen an adult look as sad as he did.

He leaned over and put an arm around each of us. "There's been a car accident," he said in a voice cracking with sorrow. "Your father is . . . was . . . killed. May he rest in peace."

I don't remember much about the next few minutes, except that I threw up my lunch in the principal's bathroom.

Anna and I held hands in the car. I didn't speak. Anna asked Grandpa Morris if he was sure that Dad was dead. Couldn't it be a mistake? Couldn't it be some other man? Grandpa Morris shook his head no.

As we turned onto our block I remembered Mom.

I thought, Our father is dead and our mother doesn't know. How could that be? I felt a wrenching in my stomach again. "Mom's at work," I told Grandpa Morris.

"Your mother is at the house," Grandpa

Morris said softly. "We picked her up at the hospital. Gram Elsie is with her." So Mom knew about Dad. She was at the hospital. Did Mom see Dad? Was he alive when she saw him? There were so many questions I wanted to ask. But if I asked them it would mean my father was really dead. So I didn't say anything.

Anna and I ran into the house. The first thing I saw was my father's bathrobe. He was standing at the sink. He wasn't dead. It was all a nightmare and now I was awake.

The person at the sink turned around. But it wasn't my father. It was my mother wearing my father's bathrobe. I felt angry at her for that, but I soon forgot my anger because I was crying and crying and crying in my Gram Elsie's arms. Anna ran to Mom and put her arms around her waist.

Our mother wrapped her arms around Anna's shoulders and looked around the room. Her eyes were red from crying and her voice seemed far away. "How could this be?" she said. "How could this be?"

CHAPTER 7

The next thing I remember was that Anna and I were sitting on the living room couch with Gram Elsie. I could hear Grandpa Morris on the phone in the kitchen, but I couldn't make out was he was saying.

"Where's Mom?" I asked.

"She's resting," Gram Elsie said. "You and Anna stay down here with me for now."

"I was supposed to play soccer this afternoon," I said to no one in particular. The words popped into my head and I just blurted them out. I felt terrible as soon as I said it. How could I think of soccer, I wondered, if my father is dead? I repeated the word over and over in my head. *Dead. Dead. Dead.* But I still couldn't believe it. I still didn't understand that my father would *never* be there for our birthday, *never* again make dinner with us, *never* laugh at one of my jokes.

A little later my father's parents and sister came in. They were all crying. They gave Anna and me big hugs, which made them cry even harder. Mom stayed in her room, but Grandmother Ruth, Grandfather David, and Aunt Judith took turns going up to see her.

Our neighbors, Mr. and Mrs. Trono, brought over a big ziti casserole, salad, a long loaf of Italian bread, and an apple pie. They said they were sorry about what happened, but they didn't stay.

I didn't think I would ever eat again. But when Gram Elsie put a plate of food in front of me, I ate it. That night, Anna and I slept in the same bed.

As soon as I opened my eyes the next morning, I remembered that Dad was dead. Anna woke up when I did and I could feel that she remembered too. We didn't say anything. We didn't have to. We knew exactly how one another felt.

On the way to the kitchen we met Grandpa Morris. He was bringing a breakfast tray up to our mother. "Come with me," he said. "Say good morning to your mother."

Mom was lying in bed. Her face was swollen from crying. She looked so sad that I felt afraid of her, just the way I was afraid of Grandpa Morris at school the day before.

"Here's a little something for you, Rachel," Grandpa Morris told her.

She shook her head and whispered, "I don't want anything, Dad."

"Drink something. Eat a little," he said. "The girls need you."

"I know," she said. Mom looked from one of us to the other. "Are you two okay?" she asked. She started crying again when she asked us that. Then she hugged us.

We stayed with Mom while she ate her breakfast. In the Jewish tradition, funerals are usually held very soon after the death. So Grandpa Morris explained that we'd all be going to Jewish Memorial Chapel for my dad's funeral service at three o'clock.

"How will I go on without him?" Mom asked.

"You will," Grandpa Morris said. He put his arm around her. "Jonathan was a splendid man," he said. "We were all blessed to have him with us."

"Did he suffer, Dad?" she asked.

"No," he said. "The doctor said death was instantaneous, remember?"

Mom nodded.

I held onto that idea for the rest of the day. Dad was dead, but he didn't suffer.

* * *

The chapel was filled with people. Many of our relatives were there. I also recognized some people that my mom and dad knew from work. Elvia and her mother, some of our teachers, and our neighbors and friends were there too. But I didn't talk to anyone. I just stayed between Anna and Gram Elsie the whole time. Grandpa Morris stayed next to my mother. She wore sunglasses and looked at the floor a lot.

I don't remember anything about the memorial service, except that a friend of my dad's from work made a speech. He said my father was one of the sweetest, most thoughtful people he'd ever known, and that his death was a great loss to the community as well as his family. Then my aunt Judith started to make a speech about Dad. But she began crying so hard in the middle of it that Grandfather David went to the front of the chapel and helped her to her seat.

After the burial we went back to our house to sit shivah for a week. That means we stayed home and people came to visit us to say they were sorry that Dad died. Both sets of grandparents stayed with us. And my aunt Judith was there most of the time too. She only went home to sleep.

Most of the people who came to see us brought food, then sat down to visit and eat.

Anna and I helped serve coffee and cake. Sometimes we loaded and unloaded the dishwasher. People smiled at us, but they looked sad at the same time. And often, when they looked at us, tears would gather in their eyes. I understood that they felt sorry for us because we were kids without a father.

Whenever people weren't at our house, Mom stayed in her room. Even when we had company, she sometimes excused herself to go back upstairs to the room she used to share with Dad. Anna and I heard her crying behind the closed door. I wanted to tell Mom about the kiss that Dad blew her the morning he died and how he said his kisses always caught up to her. But I was afraid that would just make her sadder.

Gram Elsie said we needed to leave Mom alone. That it would take time for her to feel like herself again. I knew what Gram Elsie meant, because I sure didn't feel like myself. Neither did Anna. Anna and I stayed together during the entire shivah. I was glad we had each other.

When shivah finally ended, I thought that Gram Elsie and Grandpa Morris would go home. I didn't know what would happen to us when they left. Our mother couldn't take care of Anna and me, and we didn't know how to

Our dad was gone forever.

take care of her. So I was relieved when Gram Elsie said that she and Grandpa Morris would stay for at least another week. "We'll help hold down the fort," Gram Elsie said. Grandpa Morris would go back to his office during the day and we would go to school. But Mom wasn't going back to work yet.

It felt weird to be in school after Dad died. I was sorry that Anna and I weren't in the same class anymore. Kids stared at me. I felt like yelling, "Haven't you ever seen a kid whose father died?" Then I realized that since *I* didn't know any kids my age whose father had died, they probably didn't, either. At recess I caught up with Anna. She also said she didn't like being in school.

No one asked us to play at recess. But that was all right because I didn't feel like playing anyway.

"How was school?" Gram Elsie asked after our first day back.

"Okay," I answered.

That night, no one came to visit and the five of us ate dinner together in the kitchen. Gram Elsie made Mom's favorite meat loaf. Grandpa Morris turned on the radio and tuned in a rock station. Suddenly, in the middle of the meal, Mom started to cry again. "I'm sorry," she said. "It's the radio."

I listened. The radio was playing one of Dad's favorite songs, "Stop in the Name of Love." Dad was always singing that song when he cooked.

Stop In The Name Of Love   The Supremes
Wooden Ships Crosby, Stills, Nash and Young
Voodoo Chile   Jimi Hendrix
Ramblin Rose   Grateful Dead
Everyday People Sly and the Family Stone
Fortunate Son Credence Clearwater Revival

Dad's Cooking Tunes

songs that will always remind me of the best dad in the world.

The last words of the song I heard before Gram Elsie switched it off were, " . . . before you break my heart."

My heart *is* broken, I thought, because I'll never, ever see my dad again.

CHAPTER 8

After a week, Gram Elsie and Grandpa Morris went back to their own house and Mom went back to work. Anna and I didn't bother going to our after-school activities anymore. I stopped going to Brownies. I no longer wanted to fly up to Girl Scouts. Anna didn't go back to her violin lessons. She didn't play the violin at home, either. "I don't feel like it," she said. We never played music on my dad's stereo like we used to. Anything we would've listened to would have reminded us of him.

My friends at school never mentioned anything about my dad, but I knew they felt sorry for me. And after a few days back at school, they started treating me like normal. But I didn't feel normal.

The days-without-Dad passed along until it was mid-December. Even though our lives were upset and sad without him, Anna and I were looking forward to Hanukkah.

It was a few days before the first night of Hanukkah, and we were getting dressed for school.

"Do you think we should buy a Hanukkah present for Mom?" Anna asked me.

I knew the answer without thinking about it. "No. She wouldn't want any presents now."

Anna and I went downstairs and made breakfast while Mom rushed around getting ready for work. Then she left and we walked to the bus stop.

At lunchtime that day, Elvia asked me, "Want to come to my house after school to play soccer? We have enough kids for two teams. It's really fun."

I pictured Anna going home to the empty house. I didn't want her to be alone and I didn't want to be without her. Besides, I didn't feel much like playing soccer. "No thanks," I said. "I have to go right home after school."

That afternoon, our class rehearsed for the school's winter holiday show. I hated singing happy holiday songs.

Coming home from school, a bunch of third-graders started singing "Jingle Bells" on the school bus. "If I hear 'Jingle Bells' one more time," I told Anna, "I'll re-bell."

Anna laughed. It was the first time I'd heard her laugh since Dad died. It was the first time I'd made a joke since Dad died.

When we came into the empty house, we did what we'd been doing every day since Gram Elsie and Grandpa Morris left. Anna started her homework and I watched soap operas. On the soap opera I watched that afternoon, a man was killed in a car accident. I turned off the TV.

At seven sharp, Mom walked in the door. She looked tired and sad. "Hi," she said.

"Hi," we said back.

She was walking through the kitchen to go up to her room to change.

"What's for dinner?" I asked.

"There must be some of those frozen meals left," she said. "I had a big lunch. I'm not hungry. You girls go ahead."

We never ate frozen dinners before Dad died. My parents were both sensational cooks. Mom went to school to study cooking. She even taught some cooking classes herself. Dad used to say that Mom taught him everything he knew about cooking.

There were only two frozen meals left in the

freezer. Anna took the turkey pot pie and I took the three-course baked chicken dinner. We popped them in the microwave, set the timer, and waited for it to ding.

We were eating when Mom came into the kitchen. She was wearing Dad's bathrobe again. I hated when she wore that. While we finished our so-called dinner, she put water on for tea and took out some crackers and peanut butter for herself.

I put my empty frozen food tray on top of the overflowing wastebasket. It fell off, so I stuck it in the sink with the unwashed breakfast dishes. I thought, I should put those dishes in the dishwasher. I opened the dishwasher to find that it was already full of dirty dishes. I reached under the sink for dishwasher powder. There wasn't any. I closed the dishwasher and sat down again.

Mom opened the peanut butter jar and peered inside. "This is empty," she said.

"There wasn't any cereal this morning," I told her. "So we had peanut butter sandwiches for breakfast." I remembered how stale the bread had tasted.

I looked around the kitchen. It was a mess. We were a mess. I could feel that Anna was thinking the same thing. It was as if we'd lost *both* of our parents. Our mother had to start to take control or we'd be lost too.

I stuck out a foot. "Mom," I said. "I don't have any clean socks for school. I've worn these three days in a row."

Mom was a stickler for clean underwear and socks. I figured she'd react to that.

"We'll go shopping this weekend," she said, "and buy some food and clothes."

"You mean we're never going to wash our clothes again?" I asked. "We're just going to keep buying new ones?"

"Disposable clothes," Anna mumbled. "That's disgusting."

I remembered how hard my father worked to save the environment. He had taught us from an early age that it was important not to waste things.

"Mom, what would Dad have said if he knew we were going to buy underwear because our old ones were dirty?" I asked.

Mom recoiled as if I had hit her. She never mentioned Dad to us. And we'd been careful not to talk about him in front of her. But I couldn't stop. "Dad would have hated the way things are around here," I said.

I pictured what my dad would have done if he saw the kitchen the way it was. He'd say, "Let's pull this place together. Let's make it shine." Then he'd assign us tasks, put on some soul music, and we'd sing and dance while we did dishes, wiped counters, and swept the floor.

"We have to pull this thing together," I told my mother. "Let's make it shine."

Mom folded her arms and stared at me with big, sad eyes. She knew that I was imitating Dad. Finally she spoke. "I know I have to pull *myself* together," she whispered. "I'm trying."

Anna and I didn't say anything. We waited to see what Mom would say next.

"I guess you two don't have time to keep the house organized because of all of your after-school activities," she said.

"We don't do after-school stuff anymore," I said.

Mom looked surprised. "You don't?"

"Not since Da — not for awhile," Anna told her.

"What about your violin lessons, Anna?" she asked.

Anna shook her head. "I don't want to play anymore."

"We come right home after school," I said. "But we ran out of dishwasher soap and lots of other stuff."

"We don't know how to use the washer and dryer," said Anna. "We never did it before."

"I'm sorry," Mom said in a hushed voice.

Then she sat up a little straighter and took a long sip of tea. Finally, she spoke. "Anna, find me a pad and pencil. Abby, walk around the kitchen and help me figure out what we're out of. We'll make a list." Once again, she was taking charge.

I told Mom all the stuff we needed to buy at the supermarket.

"Tomorrow," she said, "we'll go grocery shopping. Then I'm going to find someone who can be here when you girls come home from school. Someone who can cook your dinner and do some of the cleaning up. You won't have to do kitchen chores, but I'm going to teach you both how to do your own wash, okay?"

Anna and I nodded.

"I want you to start your violin lessons again next week, Anna. And back to practicing at least half an hour a day. Do you understand?"

Anna nodded.

Mom pointed at me. "And you, young lady, have you been watching television after school?"

I nodded.

"No television on weekdays. That's always been the rule in this house."

Even though Mom was scolding me, I

smiled. I was so happy to have my take-charge mom back. "Aren't you jumping up from Brownies to Girl Scouts soon?" she asked.

"It's not 'jumping up,' Mom," I said with a little laugh. "It's called 'flying up.' But I dropped out of Brownies."

"Flying up? Well, sprout some wings fast, Abby. I want you back at your Brownie meetings and I want you to become a Girl Scout."

Anna and I exchanged a small smile.

Mom stood up. "Anna, why don't you go tune your violin? You don't want to be rusty for your lesson. Abby, go get your homework and come back here with it."

A few minutes later, I was sitting at the kitchen table doing my homework. Mom was cleaning the kitchen and Anna was upstairs tuning her violin. As she was clearing the table, Mom took a bite of Anna's unfinished turkey pot pie. "This is disgusting," she said. "I'll make sure to find a housekeeper who knows how to cook."

Anna started playing a song. After the first few notes, I recognized it — "Jingle Bells." Mom made a kind of choking laugh and gave me a crooked smile. It wasn't my old mom, but it was sure better than no mom at all.

The Shooting Star

CHAPTER 9

Our family life wasn't very happy after my dad died. Things just weren't the same without him. But we did settle down to a "new" kind of family life. Or maybe I should say family lives. Mom, Anna, and I had very different interests and schedules. We were hardly ever together.

Here's what our family life was like a year after Dad died, when Anna and I were in fifth grade.

Mom became more of a workaholic than ever. That fall she was promoted to a bigger, better, and more time-consuming job at her publishing company in New York. I think she was keeping herself busy so she wouldn't miss Dad so much.

Anna spent even more time with her violin than she did before Dad died. If she didn't have a violin lesson after school, then she spent time practicing. And if she wasn't practicing, she was doing her homework at the library with her best friend, Terry.

And me? I became more and more involved in sports. I played on a soccer team and a softball team and I took tennis lessons. We had a housekeeper — Mrs. Russell — who was at our house from three o'clock until Mom came home around seven. Mrs. R. was usually alone in the house, cleaning or cooking our dinner. She was a great cook, but she wasn't there on weekends. Since Mom didn't like to cook anymore, on Saturdays and Sundays we mostly ate deli or Chinese takeout, or we went to a restaurant.

One Sunday in late November, I left the house before Anna and Mom were even up. After a morning of tennis, I ate lunch at Elvia's. We spent the rest of the day playing soccer and hanging out with the kids on her block.

Around six-thirty I came home to a dark, empty house. I didn't know where my sister and mother were or what they had been doing all day. But that wasn't unusual.

I turned on the kitchen light. There was a note stuck to the refrigerator door.

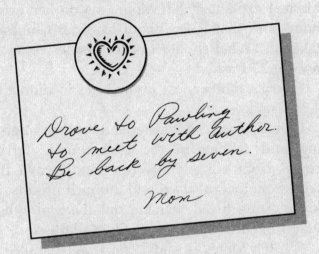

Drove to Pawling to meet with author. Be back by seven.

Mom

coming home to an empty house — again.

I was glad Mom was coming home soon and wondered what we were having for dinner.

The phone rang. It was my mother on her car phone. "I'm on Route six-eighty-four," she said, "and I'm starving."

"Me too," I told her.

"Why don't you order Chinese," she suggested, "and I'll pick it up on the way home."

"What should I order?"

"Oh, I don't know," my mother answered. "Whatever you want is fine with me."

As soon as I hung up the phone, it rang again. This time it was Anna, looking for Mom. I explained that Mom was on her way home and that I was about to order Chinese takeout. "What should I order besides sesame noodles?" I asked.

"Terry's mother just invited me to dinner," Anna said.

I could hear Terry's sister and brother laughing and talking in the background. Terry comes from a big family (the kind I envied), with a mother, a *father*, and a bunch of kids. I knew Anna loved to hang out there just the way I liked to hang out at Elvia's house.

"I'll tell Mom," I said. "She won't mind."

I ordered steamed dumplings, sesame noodles, and chicken with snow peas for Mom and me. Then I set the table with two plates and chopsticks. The house was so quiet it gave me the creeps. I was disappointed that Anna wasn't going to be home for dinner. I turned on the TV and found a sports channel with a soccer match.

Mom came in through the kitchen and poked her head into the living room. "Turn that down for a minute, will you? I have to call Steve." Steve was Mom's assistant at work.

I watched a little more of the soccer match, but my stomach kept grumbling, "Feed me." I went into the kitchen. Mom was still on the phone and eating sesame noodles right out of the carton. She gave me a weak smile and mouthed, "I'm going to be on this call for awhile. You go ahead and eat."

I took the sesame noodles from Mom and made us each a plate with half of everything. I gave her a plate and took mine back to the soccer game.

I had finished eating when Mom passed behind me on her way upstairs. "I have to edit a manuscript tonight," she said. "Did you do your homework?"

Of course I hadn't. I turned off the TV and went upstairs to face the homework I'd been putting off all weekend. I had just settled down to it when Anna came in. "Hey, Abby," she said. "Mom said to come downstairs."

I figured Mom was going to get mad at me for not cleaning up after our dinner, and I was annoyed. I had ordered the food and put it out. Couldn't she throw away a couple of cartons and put two dishes in the dishwasher without making a big deal out of it?

Mom was waiting for us at the table. I was surprised to see that the empty food cartons had been thrown away and the dishes were already in the dishwasher. "What's up?" I asked.

"Have a seat," she answered.

"Don't mind if I do," I said. I picked up the chair and headed out of the room with it. That got a laugh from Mom and Anna. I brought the chair back to the table and sat down in it. Mom looked from one of us to the other. "I haven't talked to either of you in days," she said. "I just wanted to catch up."

Just then, the phone rang. It was a business call for Mom.

The fortune cookies that came with our Chinese food lay side by side in the middle of the table. I took one and handed the other to Anna. We each opened a cookie and read our own fortunes, then one another's.

You will find happiness in your family.

Time is the best gift you can give those you love.

How could these fortunes come true if our family was never together?

86

Ten minutes later, Mom was still on the phone. Anna and I gave up and went back upstairs to our room.

Anna flopped across her bed. "Maybe we'll see Mom more during the holidays," she said.

"I doubt it," I grumbled. "It's going to be more of the same." I grabbed my notebook and held it under my arm the way Mom held the manuscripts she edited. "I know it's a holiday, girls," I said in a crisp voice that mimicked Mom's. "But I'll be going into the office for a few hours. I get so much more work done when no one else is there." I checked the time on my watch. "Have to run or I'll miss that train."

Instead of laughing, Anna looked horrified.

I turned to see Mom standing in the doorway. She gave me a weak smile, so I knew she wasn't angry at me. Then she sat down on my bed. "I — *we* — need a vacation," she said. "I've been thinking we should go away together during the holidays. I'll take off the ten days that you two have off from school."

I couldn't believe my ears. A vacation! When Dad was alive we went on camping trips every summer. We'd even been to Disney World as a family. And just a few weeks before Dad died, we took a four-day driving trip to see the fall foliage in Vermont. But we hadn't had a family vacation since then. I figured we never would.

Mom unfolded a map and laid it out in front of us.

"Florida!" Anna exclaimed.

"Are we gong to Orlando?" I asked. "This time let's go to Epcot Center!"

"We're not going to Orlando," she said. "We're going someplace quiet. A place where I can rest and be alone with you two."

I studied the map. "Are we going to Miami Beach?" I asked. "A kid in my class visits his grandparents there. He said it's really nice."

Mom shook her head no. She pointed to a tiny green island off the west coast of Florida. "We're going to this island. One of my authors went there last winter and said it would be perfect for the three of us," she said. "I'll make reservations tomorrow."

I squinted to see the small, skinny green island pointing out from the coast of Florida. " 'Sanibel,' " I read. "I've never heard of it."

"A lot of people haven't," Mom said. "That's one of the nice things about Sanibel. Besides being beautiful, it's quiet and restful."

I thought of the fortunes from the cookies. *You will find happiness in your family.* And, *Time is the best gift you can give to those you love.* Ten days alone with my mother and sister on a beautiful tropical island. I couldn't wait.

CHAPTER 10

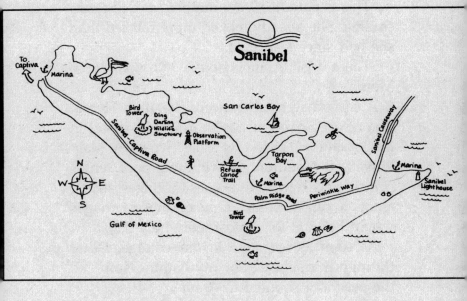

A perfect place for a family vacation.

Three weeks later, Mom, Anna, and I said good-bye to the Long Island snow and zero-degree weather. In a few hours, we were saying hello to seventy-five-degree breezes and the bright Florida sunshine. We rode in an open convertible along the one main road that ran the length of Sanibel Island. I took in a deep breath of flower-scented sea breezes.

"This is paradise," my mother said. She was smiling. She already looked more relaxed than she had since Dad died.

"There it is!" Anna shouted. "On your right, Mom."

A carved sign announced The Blue Heron. The resort looked just as beautiful as it had in the brochure. There was a big two-story main lodge and restaurant, a swimming pool, tennis courts, and twenty-five guest cottages strung along a sandy beach. One of those cottages would be ours for almost ten whole days.

As soon as we were in our cottage, I dug through my suitcase for my bathing suit. "To the beach," I shouted to Anna.

"Aren't you going to unpack first?" she asked.

"Later," I answered. "Come on, I'll race you to the water!"

"I'm going to unpack," said Anna. She'd already made a neat pile of the half dozen library books she intended to read.

I pulled on my bathing suit, tucked my hair in my baseball cap, and went to find Mom. She was in the kitchen. "Come on," I shouted happily. "Let's go to the beach!"

"I'm going to check out the golf course," she said. "I'll catch up with you later."

I went to the beach alone. A bunch of people were playing volleyball. I watched for awhile. "Want to join in?" a red-haired man called to me.

"You bet," I said.

He threw me the ball. "I'm Brad. I keep things moving around here. What's your name?"

"Abby," I shouted back to him.

"Listen up, everybody," Brad called out. "I have to go back to the sports center. Abby, here, is going to take my place. Have a good game. Drop the ball off at the sports center when you finish."

I played with Charlie and Tammy Karmorn and their aunt against three kids and their father. When we finished the game, we all ran into the sea to cool off. After that, we brought the ball back to Brad, and he gave us some beach towels. Then we headed over to the pool for a swim. What a great afternoon! I couldn't wait to tell Anna and Mom all about it.

Back at our cottage, I found Mom and Anna laid out on beach chairs by the water. Mom had fallen asleep with a manuscript on her lap and Anna was reading a book and listening to her Walkman. I went for a walk on the beach by myself.

The next morning, Mom played golf and I took a tennis lesson. Anna said she was going to hang out with Laurie, a girl staying at the cottage next to ours. "Laurie plays the piano and has a lot of classical music tapes," Anna said. "Mozart's her favorite."

The morning passed with Anna, Mom, and me busy with different activities. We weren't together for lunch, either. Anna was having a picnic with Laurie, and Mom was grabbing a bite between holes of golf.

I went to the Blue Heron deck restaurant, where Mom said I could charge my lunch. The place was packed with families, including Charlie and Tammy Karmorn. I saw that there were two younger Karmorn kids, so counting the parents and aunt they were a family of seven. The Karmorns were all laughing at something their aunt had said. They didn't even notice me.

I imagined how different our vacation would have been if Dad were still alive. How

Tennis, anyone?

we would have been one of those families having a great time together. I didn't want to sit alone in a restaurant surrounded by all those big, happy families.

A young woman stepped up to me and cheerfully asked, "How many of you will there be?"

"I'll have a sandwich to go," I told her. "A tuna sandwich."

As I left the lodge with my takeout, I passed Brad's sports center stand. He was surrounded by piles of clean beach towels, stacks of beach chairs and umbrellas, and a collection of athletic equipment.

"Hey, Abby," he said. "How's it going?"

"Great," I said. "Just great."

"We have a van going over to the Ding Darling Wildlife Refuge in half an hour. Maybe you and your folks would like to go."

I wondered if Anna and Mom would want to do that with me. Then I remembered that Anna was playing with her new friend and Mom was taking a golf lesson in the afternoon. "Not today," I told Brad.

I went back to the cottage and ate my sandwich alone. Well, I wasn't exactly alone. Anna and her new friend Laurie were hanging out on the screened-in porch. But soon after I got there, they decided to go over to the lodge and check out the books in the library room.

"Want to come with us?" Anna asked. "We'll wait until you've finished eating."

"Go to a library during vacation!?" I replied in horror. "Never!"

By the time Mom came back from golf, it was time for the Blue Heron volleyball game.

"I have to go," I told Mom when she came in.

"That's okay," she said. "I have to go over to the lodge and fax something to Steve. You have fun."

Later, as I floated on my back in the pool, I thought, The pool is wonderful and I feel great from all the exercise I've been getting. And I *am* having fun. Tears came into my eyes. But it's not the vacation we planned. We took this vacation to be together and we're not really together. We're not acting like a family. I rolled over and dove under the water to wash away my tears.

The next day, when I went to pick up my solitary take-out lunch, Brad called, "Hey, how's it going?" like he always did.

"Great," I said, like I always did.

I wondered what new activity he'd propose that my mother and sister wouldn't want to do with me.

"So," he said, "you and your folks joining

us for the Family Night New Year's party?"

A nighttime activity. Maybe we could do that. After all, Mom couldn't play golf at night, and Laurie would be with her own family for New Year's Eve. Brad told me all about the party. It sounded perfect.

"I'll ask my mom," I told Brad. I grabbed a towel and headed toward the cottages. "Hey," I called over my shoulder. "Thanks." I couldn't wait to tell Mom and Anna about the Family Night New Year's party.

Anna and Mom were on the beach. Mom's eyes were closed and she was listening to her Walkman. Anna had on her Walkman too, and was reading a book. I knelt in the sand in front of them and waved my arms to get their attention.

They came out of their separate worlds and smiled dreamily at me.

"Hi," Anna said.

"Hi," Mom said. "What's up?"

"Great news," I told them. "There's a *family* New Year's party with a big dinner and entertainment and even dancing. Brad's signing people up. Can we go?"

"Laurie and her family are going," Anna said. "It sounds like fun."

"Okay," Mom said. She closed her eyes again.

I grabbed her hand. "Let's all go sign up now."

"Abby, you do it for us," Mom suggested. "I'm sooo comfortable."

"Mom, I'm sick of doing everything alone. Can't we go over there and sign up together?"

Mom looked disappointed. "Aren't you having a good vacation?" she asked.

"I am," I protested. "I really am. And there're lots of kids for me to play sports with. But I just thought . . . I don't know . . . couldn't we all . . ."

Anna was picking up my vibes on our twin wavelength. She grabbed Mom's other hand. "Come on," she said. "Let's go."

We pulled Mom out of her chair. None of us spoke on the way to the lodge. We were in our own worlds. Mom was probably thinking about a manuscript. Anna was still listening to her Walkman. And I was wondering if I'd ever feel like I was part of a real family again.

When we reached the lodge, Mom walked to Brad's stand.

"I would like to sign up my family for the New Year's party," she said.

He looked at her with surprise. "Oh," he said. "I didn't know you were here with a family. I thought you were alone."

Mom looked hurt and confused. "I'm here

with my girls," she said. Anna and I ran up beside her.

Brad looked from Anna to me. "Twins!" he exclaimed. "I thought you two were the same person. I've never seen you together before."

Brad turned the sign-up sheet around for Mom to sign. "You'll have a great time at the party." He grinned at Anna and me. "You sure did have me fooled."

As soon as we were out of earshot, Mom said, "I can't believe he didn't know we were together," she said. "Isn't it his job to keep track of people?"

"Mom, we're *never* together!" I exclaimed. "We do different things *all* day long! How would he know?"

I felt ashamed for yelling. I didn't want to ruin the vacation for Anna and Mom. But I had said it and it was too late to take it back.

CHAPTER 11

Mom took us each by the hand. "Come on," she said. "Let's go someplace where we can talk quietly."

"How about the deck restaurant," Anna suggested. "Lots of families eat there. I see them all the time."

I gave Anna a grateful smile. I wasn't the only one who had missed being a family.

"To the deck," Mom said.

A few minutes later, we were drinking pink lemonade, but none of us knew what to say. Finally, Mom spoke. "I wanted you to have a good time on this vacation," she said.

"We are!" Anna and I exclaimed in unison.

"It's just that we . . ." Anna began.

" . . . thought we'd spend more time together," I said, completing the sentence for her.

Anna and I smiled at one another. We hadn't talked together like that in a long time.

"We see all these other families doing things together," I explained. "It doesn't feel like we're a family."

Mom looked hurt by that, but she understood what I meant. "I see those families too," she said. "It reminds me of all the wonderful times we used to have. I find it upsetting, with Jon not here."

"We're still a family," I said. "A new kind of family."

"Abby, I don't think I can handle that big party at the lodge," Mom said.

"We don't have to go," I said. "As long as we do *something* together."

Mom and Anna decided that we should spend New Year's Eve day as a family. That night, at dinner, we wrote up our daytime activities for our special Stevenson New Year's celebration.

We started our New Year's Eve morning by going for a walk on the beach. Mom pointed to the sea. "Look! Porpoises!" she exclaimed.

Three porpoises were swimming and playing a hundred feet or so from the shoreline. We watched their dark shapes gracefully leaping and diving.

"Come on," I shouted. "Let's keep up with them."

New Years Eve Schedule

Morning
Walk on beach
Bike ride

Afternoon
Tour of Ding Darling Wildlife Sanctuary
Swim and rest at pool

Evening
Make dinner together and eat by pool
On beach at midnight

Our first family celebration without Dad.

We held hands and ran along the beach. When the porpoises swam out to sea, we watched them until they were out of sight. Then we went into the ocean for a swim. Anna and I did great porpoise dives for Mom.

After that, we rented bikes and rode along a trail that led to the wildlife refuge. On the way, we stopped at an outdoor restaurant for lunch. During lunch, Anna read to us from a guide book about the history of the wildlife refuge and all the cool things we would be seeing there.

After lunch, we rode our bikes through the refuge. We took our time and stopped to read signs and observe the animals and birds. We saw alligators and a crocodile and a zillion birds. I imitated how some of the birds walked and ate, which cracked up Mom and Anna. We were having a lot of fun together.

Back at the Blue Heron, we jumped in the pool. After a swim we all fell asleep in the beach chairs. Then we swam again to wake up. At six o'clock we went to our cottage to prepare a special New Year's Eve dinner.

We had decided to cook on the gas grill by the pool. We cut up fish and vegetables and put them on skewers. Then Mom made a tasty sauce to go with the fish and Anna and I concocted a punch. We wrote down our recipe.

As the sun set, we sat facing the ocean, sipping our drinks and listening to our dinner hiss on the grill.

Mom took a long sip of her drink. "We should give this punch a name," she said.

"Let's call it New Year's punch," I said, punching the air.

"And let's always have it on New Year's Eve," added Anna.

"Perfect," said Mom with a satisfied smile. "What else can we do *every* New Year's Eve?"

> Abby's and Anna's New Year's Punch
>
> 4 parts Fresh squeezed Orange Juice
>
> 1 Part Cranberry Juice
>
> 2 Parts Ginger Ale

One of our New Year's Eve traditions.

"Make dinner together," said Anna.

"And grill it no matter where we are and whatever the weather is like," I said. "Even if there's four feet of snow."

Mom patted me on the arm. "That's the sort of thing your father would have said."

"He was really into that tradition stuff, wasn't he?" I asked.

Mom nodded.

"Remember how every Fourth of July we had to eat that cold tomato soup?" I said.

"Gazpacho," Mom said. "And those *awful*

103

hot dogs. He insisted we have the brand he ate on July Fourth when he was a kid."

"I liked the potato salad," Anna said. "And how we always played badminton after the picnic."

"Even in the rain!" I shrieked. "Remember?" We all cracked up remembering the Fourth of July when Dad insisted we play badminton in a torrential downpour.

"The birdie couldn't make it over the net. It kept getting beaten down by the rain," Mom giggled.

"That birdie deserves to live in the Ding Darling Wildlife Refuge for the rest of its life," I told them. Anna and Mom laughed. I pictured the plastic shuttlecock perched on a reed at the edge of the lagoon amidst herons and short-billed downwichers.

Mom spoke in a soft, sad voice. "Before you girls were born, your father and I talked about how we would have lots of family traditions for you two. That we would celebrate holidays in ways that would be special and memorable and that would be repeated year after year."

Anna and I nodded. We wanted her to go on talking about the past, when our father was alive.

"I liked how we did those things," I said.

"But now that your father's gone, I can't

bear to do all the things we did with him. Not yet. It's too painful." Her voice choked up on those last words. "It's a little easier, being here in new surroundings. But still . . ." Her voice trailed off.

I patted her arm. "That's okay, Mom," I said. "We can start new traditions. And this time Anna and I can help figure out what they should be."

"Maybe we could still do *some* of the things we did with Jon," my mother said.

"Remember how we always shared New Year's resolutions," said Anna. "Maybe we could keep that tradition."

"Dad's first resolution always was, 'I will not lose one pair of glasses this year,' " I said.

Anna giggled. "That's a resolution he could never keep."

"And you, Miss Abby," Mom said, pretending to be cross, "always resolving to do your homework early on the weekends."

"That's a tough one to keep too," I said.

"Let's do resolutions again tonight," said Anna. "And every New Year's Eve from now on."

Suddenly Mom jumped up and screeched, "The grill! We forgot." We ran to the grill to see what remained of our dinner. The fish was so overcooked that it was dry as cardboard.

The onions and peppers were black, and the mushrooms were shriveled up to the size of peas.

Mom looked disappointed, but I started to laugh. "Is it going to be a new tradition that we have to ruin the dinner on New Year's Eve?" I asked.

"No," Mom said. "Absolutely not. But it may be a new tradition that I take you out to a restaurant on New Year's Eve. Let's see if we can crash the Blue Heron party. I feel enough like a family with my two girls to handle that scene."

So we threw away the ruined meal and changed into our best dresses. "Don't forget those resolutions," Mom yelled to us from her bedroom. "I can't wait to hear them later."

"You too, Mom," I yelled back.

When we arrived at the lodge, the guests were already choosing dessert from the big buffet. The waitress said she still had a table for three available, and that there was plenty of food left. Then she told us to have fun.

A reggae band was playing and a buffet was piled high with Caribbean foods. Even though it wasn't midnight, everyone was wishing everyone else "Happy New Year." Charlie and Tammy Karmorn came over to our table. I introduced them to my mother and sister. They were cool and didn't go on and on about Anna and me being twins.

Then, on the way to the dessert table, we stopped to say hello to Laurie's family.

After dinner, there was entertainment — a juggling act, a barbershop quartet, an acrobat, and more reggae music.

We decided not to stay in the lodge for the midnight celebration. We wanted to be alone — just the three of us — on the beach, as we had planned. So at eleven-thirty we headed back to our cottage, wrapped ourselves in blankets, and lay on the sand watching the stars.

At midnight we wished each other "Happy New Year" and shared our resolutions. Anna resolved to practice her violin even more than she already did. I resolved to do my homework earlier on the weekends. Mom resolved not to rush around so much and not to talk on the phone during dinner. And we all had one resolution in common: We would spend more time together.

"Dinner at home, just we three, every Wednesday and Sunday night," Mom said.

"When Abby has a big game after school, I'll watch her play, unless I have a violin lesson," said Anna.

"And when I'm having trouble with home-

Together at last.

work, I'll ask Anna to help me and not be grumpy about it," I said.

After the resolutions, we hugged and wished each other "Happy New Year" again. Then we lay back and watched the stars some more. I was thinking about Dad. I was sure that Mom and Anna were too.

Dad, wherever you are, I prayed, *we remember you and miss you with all of our hearts. But we are going to be okay. We're still a family.*

Just then, a shooting star streaked across the night sky.

New Places, New Faces

CHAPTER 12

Except for my
resolution about week-
end homework, Mom,
Anna, and I kept the
New Year's resolutions
we made on Sanibel
Island. We still followed
our separate interests,
but we started to
pay more attention to
one another. Sometimes,
after dinner, Anna
would play the violin
for Mom and me.
When I had a soccer
match or softball
game on Saturday,
Anna and Mom
would show up to cheer
me on for at least part
of it. And at dinner, Mom
would often tell Anna and
me the plot of a novel
one of her authors was
working on and ask
our opinion. She
called us her junior
editors.

On the next three New Year's Eves, we made a special dinner together, drank our New Year's punch, and shared our New Year's resolutions.

The New Year's Eve Anna and I were in the seventh grade, Mom's resolution was: I will make a big change in my life.

"What kind of change?" I asked.

"I don't know, Abby," she answered. "I just know I have to do something to make my life better. I've been in a rut of unhappiness since . . ." Her voice trailed off. Mom still hardly ever talked about Dad.

Anna and I exchanged a glance. Our mother's sadness wasn't lifting and we felt bad about it. Later, alone in our room, we talked it over.

"Mom must miss Dad even more than we do," Anna said.

"I wonder what the big change will be," I added.

"And how it will affect us."

"Do you think she'll get married again?" I asked, horrified.

"I don't think so. She's so upset about Dad. No one can replace him."

"That's for sure."

So Anna and I began that new year wondering what Mom would do to change her life — which we knew would also mean *our* lives.

Looking back on that winter and spring, I can see now that there were a lot of clues to the big change Mom would finally announce to us that June.

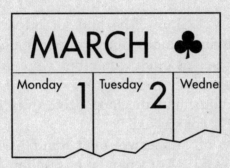

Clue #1: Late one night, as I walked by Mom's closed bedroom door, I heard her talking on the phone with her best friend, Amy Burke. "It's been more than four years, Amy, and I still feel so sad. I've been thinking that if I could get away from all these familiar places, I wouldn't be so lonely."

Just then, Anna started tuning up her violin and I couldn't hear any more of Mom's end of the phone conversation.

Clue #2: Gram Elsie and Grandpa Morris were having Sunday dinner at our house. They came to see us often when they were living on Long Island.

"Do you mind the long drive over here to see us?" Mom asked.

"Why, of course we don't mind," Grandpa Morris said. "We enjoy our Sunday drives. We'd drive twice as far and think nothing of it."

Mom smiled. "I'm glad to hear that," she said.

Clue #3: When I came home from soccer practice one afternoon, our housekeeper, Mrs. Russell, handed me a list of phone messages. One was for Anna from her violin teacher. The second message was for Mom. It was from a real estate agent in Connecticut.

Kristy and the rest of the Baby-sitters Club members would have put those first three clues together and known Mom's big change was going to be a move to Connecticut. But at the time, I didn't have a clue about how those clues fit together.

Clue #4: The evening after the real estate agent's call, Mom announced that we were going to spend Sunday visiting her friend Amy in Stamford, Connecticut.

Amy and her teenage daughter, Alexandra, took us to lunch at an outdoor cafe in Stoneybrook. Mom loved that Sunday visit to Connecticut. "Look at this wonderful town." "Isn't the shopping district just perfect?" "Aren't the houses beautiful?" "Look at those lovely hills!"

Clue #5: After lunch, Alexandra took Anna and me shopping at a mall in Stamford while Mom and Amy went off by themselves. We hung around the mall for a couple of hours and then went back to the Burkes' house to hook up with Mom. But she and Amy weren't there. When they came in a little later, Mom was glowing with excitement.

"Where were you?" I asked.

Mom hesitated, then answered, "Shopping." Amy and Mom exchanged a glance and broke into giggles.

I didn't ask Mom what she was shopping for. If I had, I wonder if she'd have answered, "A new house."

Clue #6: One night, before going to bed, Anna and I had a familiar argument.

Anna tripped over my tennis shoes (that I admit were on her side of the room). When she regained her balance, she shouted, "Can't you keep your shoes in the closet? I'm always tripping over your sneakers."

"They're *tennis* shoes," I shouted back. "Keep it straight. I have *tennis* shoes, *soccer* shoes, and *cleats* for softball."

"And *running* shoes and *regular* sneakers," she added. "Five pairs. And they all stink and they are always in my way."

Mom came in. I thought she'd get mad at us for shouting, or would try to mediate our dispute. Instead, she just smiled and said, "This house has become too small for us. You two should each have your own room."

Clue #7: On Saturday night we were settling down to watch a movie on the VCR. I was about to put in the tape when Mom asked, "Are you girls as sick of this furniture as I am?"

I looked around. There was the comfy blue couch Anna and I usually sat on and had known all our lives, the flower-patterned love seat where Mom liked to sit, and Dad's leather easy chair. None of us ever sat in Dad's chair. I felt sad just looking at it. "Our furniture is okay, Mom," I said.

"It's getting pretty tired looking," Mom told us. "And I'm tired of looking at it. I'd like to give away everything — all of our furniture — and have a fresh start."

Two weeks after Clue #7, we ate Saturday dinner at our favorite Italian restaurant.

As soon as we'd put in our orders, Mom said, "Girls, I have a big announcement to make."

Anna's eyes opened wide in alarm. My chest tightened. What would Mom's announcement be? A boyfriend? A new job?

"You may have guessed already," she said.

Anna and I shook our heads no.

Mom looked surprised that we hadn't put together the hints she'd been dropping left and right. "Well, then," she began, "you know I find it difficult to continue living in the town that holds so many memories of life with your father."

We nodded. It was then that I finally realized what her announcement would be.

"I've decided we should leave Long Island. I've bought us a house in Connecticut. In Stoneybrook, to be exact. You know, the town where we ate lunch with Amy and Alexandra. It's a wonderful house, girls. I can't wait to show it to you."

I instantly hated the idea of moving and I knew, without looking at Anna, that she felt the same way I did — terrible.

CHAPTER 13

"Why do we have to leave Long Island?" Anna asked.

"I think it will be good for us to start over in a new place," Mom answered.

"But I don't want to leave Old Woodbury," I exclaimed. "We've lived here all of our lives. What about our school and our friends?"

"And my violin lessons with Randal," added Anna. Tears filled her eyes. "What about the orchestra?"

Mom's smile turned to a frown. "I guess I should have broken it to you more gently," she said. "But the fact is, I can't go on living here. I'm so unhappy in this town. Every place I go to, everything I see, holds too many memories."

None of us said anything for a few seconds. We were all thinking about Dad. I knew how Mom felt. Lots of things about Old Woodbury made me sad too. When I passed Mario's, I'd often think, This was Dad's favorite pizza parlor. We'd be shopping in Sprouts, the produce market, and I'd remember how every time we shopped there Dad said, "Sprouts has the best fruits and vegetables this side of Sunrise Highway." And I could never go by the brick building Dad worked in without thinking about him. Mom was right about the memories.

I also thought about how lighthearted and happy Mom was on Sanibel. That was a place she'd never visited with Dad. Maybe Mom was right. Maybe we should live in a new town.

Anna and I sent a silent signal to one another not to complain in front of Mom anymore about moving. Instead, we tried to smile and seem interested as she showed us pictures of the house she'd picked out for us. It was about twice the size of the one we were living in.

"That must be so expensive," Anna said. "Can we afford it?"

"That's my other surprise," Mom said.

I held my breath. Mom sure was full of surprises.

She grinned from ear to ear. "I've gotten another promotion — and a very big raise."

"All *right*, Mom!" I cheered. "You're the best."

"Don't you see, girls," Mom said. "A new job, a new house in a new town. It can be a new life for all of us."

When we were back in our room and alone, Anna grabbed her old teddy bear, Stubbles, and held him to her chest. "I don't want a new life," she said through tears.

"Me neither," I admitted. "But maybe it won't be so bad. It'll be a fresh start."

"We'll be the new kids in school," said Anna. "That's awful. I hate meeting new people."

I understood how Anna felt, but I was actually starting to get a little excited about moving. I lay awake late into the night, wondering what it would be like to have my own room, to live in a big house in the "charming" town of Stoneybrook, and to be able to have a fresh start in life.

The next night, I went to a sleepover at Elvia's with our other best friends, Jennifer and Joyce. That's when I broke the news to them.

"You're moving?" shrieked Elvia. "But you can't. That's *awful*."

"What about your Bat Mitzvahs?" Jennifer moaned. We were all starting to think about our Bat Mitzvahs. A Bat Mitzvah is the Jewish ceremony celebrating a girl becoming an adult. It's a big deal and something I'd expected to share with my best friends.

"We are supposed to go to high school together and everything," wailed Joyce.

"We're not moving that far away," I told them. "My grandparents are going to come visit us all the time. You can too. And I'll come back. I bet there's a train or something I can take."

That made us all feel a little better. But not for long. Soon my friends actually started to cry, and to tell the truth, so did I.

Over the next two months my feelings were on a roller-coaster ride. One minute I'd be super excited about the move, the next, I'd be depressed about it.

To make matters worse, Mom sprung another surprise on us during dinner one Wednesday night. "We're going to sell our furniture and buy all new things." (Remember Clue #7?)

"You mean we're not going to bring our stuff to the new house?" I asked.

"We're selling every piece of it," Mom said. "They gave me a bonus with my promotion and I'm putting it into new furniture. New *everything!* I've hired a decorator to help us."

"Can't I keep my music stand and desk?" Anna asked.

"Of course you can keep your music stand," Mom told her. "But wouldn't you like a new desk — a bigger one with a pull-out shelf for your computer keyboard?"

"I guess," said Anna cautiously.

"Our decorator is Sylvia Steinert. She's coming here on Saturday to meet you girls. She wants to get a feel for what you're like. She'll bring pictures of furniture, paint chips, and wallpaper samples. With your help, she'll decorate your rooms."

I laughed out loud. "Everything new! Mom, that's so crazy."

I was excited about meeting the decorator. Anna wasn't. But when the day came, we both loved looking through catalogues of furniture, samples of wallpaper and rugs, and fabric swatches for curtains. It's really fun to design the room of your dreams. Anna and I would each have a room bigger than the single one we shared now.

Anna picked out a four-poster bed and flowered wallpaper. She would have a big desk plus a special cabinet for her stereo (another new purchase) and her collection of classical compact discs and sheet music.

I picked out striped paper in shades of tan, blue, and gray. My room was going to be so big that the decorator said I had room for a couch in it. I told her I wanted a convertible couch so I'd have an extra bed for my Long Island friends when they came to visit.

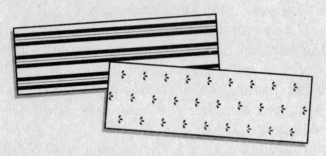

Anna and I choose wallpaper for our rooms.

Mom told the decorator to do whatever she wanted with the master bedroom. I guess she was remembering that she wouldn't be sharing this new room with Dad and didn't want to think about it too much.

But for me, Saturday was an up day on the roller-coaster ride. I enjoyed picking out stuff for my new room. Then Sunday brought a fast swoop downward. A man from a secondhand furniture store went through our house. He would take everything away the day before

we moved, including Dad's chair. Meanwhile, there was a big FOR SALE sign on the
front lawn and people were tramping through
our house with real estate agents. Definitely a
downer.

During those summer months before the
move to Stoneybrook, I went to a day camp,
where we played sports all day long. Anna
went to a sleepover camp for young musi-
cians. So it was just Mom and me getting
ready for the big move.

Late one Saturday afternoon, I found Mom
taking all of our good dishes out of the dining
room cupboard. "Are we having a party?" I
asked.

"No," she said. "I'm giving them to your
Aunt Judith. We're buying new ones. Do you
think Elvia's mother would like my copper
cooking pots?"

"Mom," I shrieked, "you can't give *everything* away. Please! I love those copper
pots."

Mom laughed. "You're right," she said. "I'm
getting carried away."

I decided then and there that my big re-
sponsibility that summer was to keep Mom
from selling or giving away everything we

Clue # 8 !

owned. I won a few. I lost a few. But when it was finally the week of our move, we still had quite a few boxes to pack and move. To our new house, in our new town, where we would begin our new life.

CHAPTER 14

The night before we moved, our friends threw a joint party for Anna and me. They gave Anna a boxed set of violin concertos on CDs as a going-away present. And they gave me a collection of balls — a soccer ball, ten cans of tennis balls, and five softballs. Everyone at the party autographed two of the softballs and the cover of Anna's CD box.

We all felt sad, but I made sure we still had fun. I told every joke I could remember — including my whole collection of elephant jokes and lightbulb jokes. It was an Abby joke-a-thon. I figured it was better for us to laugh until we cried than to just plain cry.

The next morning, movers came and put the stuff we hadn't sold or given away into a medium-sized moving van. Then Mom, Anna, and I climbed into our new minivan and said good-bye to Old Woodbury, Long Island. Mom still seemed happy about the move. But Anna was depressed and slumped beside me in the backseat. Feelingwise, I was someplace between them.

When we were pulling out of our driveway for the last time, I whispered, "Good-bye, house." As soon as I said it, I remembered our favorite childhood book — *Goodnight, Moon* — and began a litany of good-byes.

"Good-bye, street."

"Good-bye, bus stop."

"Good-bye, grocery store."

"Good-bye, dog who always poops on the sidewalk."

Anna gave a little laugh at that last one, but I knew she was still sad. I kept up the good-bye game until Mom and Anna joined in.

"Good-bye, Georgio's Pizza," Anna said.

"Good-bye, post office," Mom shouted out the window.

I still felt a little sad about saying good-bye to my familiar life, but as we drove onto the Long Island Expressway, I was already looking forward to saying hello to my new life.

The instant we turned onto Main Street in Stoneybrook, Connecticut, I sneezed. Within seconds I was having a major attack of aller-

A GREAT FAMILY TRADITION FOR OVER 50 YEARS!

Georgio's Pizza

Old Woodbury NY 555-1112

Good-bye, pizza parlor.
Good-bye, old life.

gies. I try not to think too much about being allergic to a zillion things that are part of life on Planet Earth. I believe with all my heart that I will outgrow my allergies. But it sure didn't happen the day of our big move. My runny nose and congested lungs wouldn't let me forget for a second that I have serious allergies.

Ah-choo! It was my fifth sneeze in a row. I sounded like machine gun fire.

"Mom, Abby's allergic to Stoneybrook," said Anna. "We have to go back to Old Woodbury."

Mom laughed. "Abby has allergic reactions when she's under a lot of stress," Mom explained. "Moving is stressful."

132

Hello, new house.
Hello, new life.

"That's right," I managed to say before another rush of sneezes rocked the minivan.

The first thing I noticed as we drove onto our new street was that all of the houses were big and expensive looking and had large yards.

"Which one is ours?" asked Anna.

Mom pointed to a beautiful house with a wraparound porch and a great wooden front door. "That one. Isn't it spectacular?"

Our new house *was* spectacular and just as big as the other houses on the block.

"Whose house is that?" I asked Mom as I stepped down from the minivan, and noticed the house two doors away. It was noticeable because of the number of toys in the yard.

"The real estate agent told me that a big extended family lives there," Mom answered. (Only later would I learn what the agent meant by "big.")

The moving van, which was right behind us, also pulled up to the house. While the movers started unloading boxes, Mom, Anna, and I ran inside. It was weird and wonderful to see all the furniture we'd picked out from little photos in catalogues. Couches, chairs, tables, and lamps were life-size and in the place we would call home. Anna and Mom checked out the house at a dignified pace. I ran excitedly from room to room. I yelled to my mom that the lights weren't working. She said they'd be coming on soon, that she had told Sylvia to take care of it. Even without the lights on I could see that our new house was terrific.

On the first floor were a huge living room, a family room, a big sunny kitchen, a dining room, a den, and a bathroom. Upstairs were an office for Mom, five bedrooms, and *three* baths. Mom's bedroom was actually two rooms. And Anna and I each had our own bathroom. My bedroom — my very own bedroom — was perfect! *Ah-choo*, a*h-choo*, *ah-choo*, I sneezed at my new room.

Even if I was excited and happy, it was still stressful to make a big move. It was also September, the month when my allergies are always at their worst.

I ran downstairs and back outside to help the movers. That's when I first met Kristy Thomas, resident of the house two doors away. She looked like a pretty ordinary person.

Other neighbors, the Papadakises, came to meet us and give us a big platter of food. Then Sylvia Steinert pulled into our driveway. We congratulated her on a great job, but she didn't pay much attention to our compliments and seemed disappointed to see us.

"You said you were arriving tomorrow," she

told our mother. Mom explained that we'd decided to come a day early because of her work schedule and that she'd told her assistant to tell Sylvia's assistant. But Sylvia had never received the message.

"All the utilities are scheduled to be turned on tomorrow," she announced. "Phones, electricity, water, gas. You won't have any of it until then. I'm sorry."

Sylvia was a lot more upset by this news than we were. We didn't care. Especially when Kristy's mother invited us to dinner and to stay overnight at their house.

It was great fun to meet the noisy Thomas-Brewer clan — all ten of them. They reminded me of the happy families I had envied on Sanibel Island, only theirs was bigger. There was just one problem with our dinner and sleepover at the mansion. I was allergic to just about everything in that place, including the dinner they'd made for us. But I still had fun. So did Mom. She got along great with Mrs. Brewer. Even Anna was looking happy.

As for me, I was so excited about my new life in Stoneybrook that I was practically jumping out of my skin. So I did what I always do when I'm excited. I made a lot of not very good jokes, mostly about my allergies. ("My nose is running, but don't worry, nobody can catch it.") The younger kids in Kristy's extended family seemed to like me, but I could tell Kristy thought I was a little over the top. She liked Anna better, which was pretty weird since it was obvious from the beginning that Kristy and I — both being extroverted athletes — had way more in common than Kristy and Anna did.

The next morning we ate a big breakfast in the kitchen, then went off for our first day of school in Stoneybrook. Kristy and Anna sat together on the school bus, but I sat with a bunch of kids I didn't know. I liked them right away and I could tell they liked me. I didn't let myself think about my old life during those first few days in Stoneybrook. I was too busy making new friends.

Making friends with Kristy was a lot of work. Even though I'd seen her roll her eyes and grimace at some of my jokes, I knew I could make her laugh. So I worked on my material and polished up my style. Every day I tried to make her laugh one more time than the day before.

Since Kristy loved sports, I let her know that I did too. "Any time you want to toss a ball around, I'm ready," I told her. "Just give a call, we'll have a ball."

Kristy made a face at my corny pun. She men-

Kristy Thomas was one of the few
things in Stoneybrook that
didn't make me sneeze.

tioned that a kid she baby-sat for was always rhyming. Then Kristy invited me to help out with coaching her softball team of little kids.

And here's the most exciting thing of all — Anna and I were invited to become members of the Baby-sitters Club! I told the club members that I was thrilled that they asked me and I'd love to join. I couldn't have been happier.

Anna was happy they invited her to join too, but she turned the invitation down. I could see by Kristy's expression that she was shocked that Anna didn't want to be a member of the BSC. I was a little surprised myself. But when Anna explained that she wanted to devote all of her time to music, we understood.

During those first weeks, Anna adjusted to our move too. She found a new violin teacher whom she liked as much as Randal. And she was asked to play first chair in the school orchestra. Anna also discovered that she had a lot in common with Shannon Kilbourne.

So, this is the end of my autobiography. All in all, I'd say my life has been pretty interesting. I have had one great sorrow, but I've also had lots of good times. I think my dad would be happy to see how we're all doing in our new life. I want to be someone he would be proud of — and someone who could make him laugh.

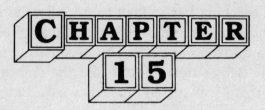

CHAPTER 15

I finished my autobiography late Sunday night. I'd never worked so hard on an assignment in my whole life.

On the way to school on Monday morning I was the quiet twin. I was still thinking about the things I'd written and wondering what my English teacher, Ms. Belcher, would think of my book. Would she think it was too sad because I wrote so much about my dad's death? Well, if she did, I thought, that would just be too bad. Because it *is* sad that my dad died when I was only nine, and it's *my* autobiography.

After I turned in my book, I tried not to think about all the things I'd written. But I couldn't help it. I'd stirred up memories that kept returning.

That night, before going to bed, I went into Anna's room. "Do you think we still look alike?" I asked.

She looked at me as if I were crazy. "What made you think of *that?*"

"I was just wondering if our hair was the same and if we dressed alike, would we look identical? Like when we were little?"

"You mean like those twins in the shopping mall?" she said.

"You remember them too!"

"Are you kidding? I even wrote about them in my autobiography."

"Me too," I told her. "What else did you write about?"

Anna handed me her autobiography. It was called *The Music of My Life.* "I titled the chapters with musical terms," she explained. "The part when we were born is called 'Lullaby.' The chapter after that is about being twins. I named it 'Duet.' " She lowered her eyes and added, "And the chapter about Dad is called 'Requiem.' "

I flipped to the back of the book to see Anna's grade. I wasn't surprised to see that she'd received an A.

"Let's see if we look alike," she whispered.

So we both put on white T-shirts, jeans, and baseball caps. I bunched my hair up under my cap so it would look like it was the same length as Anna's. Then we stood side by side and gazed at ourselves in her mirror.

"Your skin is darker," Anna commented.

"That's because I'm outside more than you are," I told her. I pointed to the scar over my eyebrow. "And I have this."

Anna noticed that I looked taller than she did. We decided that was because I was more muscular and stood straighter. "And my arms are a little more built up from playing sports," I noted. "But our faces still look the same."

"I don't mind when people mix us up now," Anna said. "It doesn't happen that often."

"I don't mind being confused with you, either," I admitted.

We didn't say it out loud, but we were both thinking, You're better than a best friend. You are my twin.

Just then, Mom came in to say good night to us. "Look at you two!" she exclaimed. "How strange to see you looking *so much* alike. What's going on?" We told her that we were seeing if we could still look identical.

"You girls have become so different from one another that I hardly even think of you as twins anymore," Mom said.

"We're still alike in a lot of ways," I said. I pulled off the baseball cap to let my hair free, and put my glasses back on.

"Well, I have to work on this manuscript before I go to sleep," she said. She checked her watch. "See you in the morning."

I ran to Mom and gave her a hug. "Well, well," she said, "what's this for?"

"For you," I said. Mom gave me a little squeeze back. Then we went to our rooms.

I went to bed happy that I was part of my family, even if it was small. We'd been through terrible times and survived. We were three strong women and I was proud of us. Even if Ms. Belcher didn't give me a good grade for my autobiography, I knew that it was A-OK.

Fortunately, so did Ms. Belcher.

J B

STONEYBROOK MIDDLE SCHOOL

A-

Splendid work, Abby. You write in a clear, concise style. I'm particularly impressed with how well you write dialogue. Reading your autobiography was a wonderful way for me to meet your family—including your father. Welcome to Stoneybrook!

J.B.

Ann M. Martin

About the Author

ANN MATTHEWS MARTIN was born on August 12, 1955. She grew up in Princeton, NJ, with her parents and her younger sister, Jane.

Although Ann used to be a teacher and then an editor of children's books, she's now a full-time writer. She gets the ideas for her books from many different places. Some are based on personal experiences. Others are based on childhood memories and feelings. Many are written about contemporary problems or events.

All of Ann's characters, even the members of the Baby-sitters Club, are made up. (So is Stoneybrook.) But many of her characters are based on real people. Sometimes Ann names her characters after people she knows, other times she chooses names she likes.

In addition to the Baby-sitters Club books, Ann Martin has written many other books for children. Her favorite is *Ten Kids, No Pets* because she loves big families and she loves animals. Her favorite Baby-sitters Club book is *Kristy's Big Day*. (By the way, Kristy is her favorite baby-sitter!)

Ann M. Martin now lives in New York with her cats, Gussie and Woody. Her hobbies are reading, sewing, and needlework — especially making clothes for children.

Read all the books
about **Abby**
in the Baby-sitters Club series
by Ann M. Martin

100 (and more)
Reasons to Stay Friends Forever!

More titles... ▶

The Baby-sitters Club titles continued...

❑ MG48226-2	#82	Jessi and the Troublemaker	$3.99
❑ MG48235-1	#83	Stacey vs. the BSC	$3.50
❑ MG48228-9	#84	Dawn and the School Spirit War	$3.50
❑ MG48236-X	#85	Claudi Kishi, Live from WSTO	$3.50
❑ MG48227-0	#86	Mary Anne and Camp BSC	$3.50
❑ MG48237-8	#87	Stacey and the Bad Girls	$3.50
❑ MG22872-2	#88	Farewell, Dawn	$3.50
❑ MG22873-0	#89	Kristy and the Dirty Diapers	$3.50
❑ MG22874-9	#90	Welcome to the BSC, Abby	$3.99
❑ MG22875-1	#91	Claudia and the First Thanksgiving	$3.50
❑ MG22876-5	#92	Mallory's Christmas Wish	$3.50
❑ MG22877-3	#93	Mary Anne and the Memory Garden	$3.99
❑ MG22878-1	#94	Stacey McGill, Super Sitter	$3.99
❑ MG22879-X	#95	Kristy + Bart = ?	$3.99
❑ MG22880-3	#96	Abby's Lucky Thirteen	$3.99
❑ MG22881-1	#97	Claudia and the World's Cutest Baby	$3.99
❑ MG22882-X	#98	Dawn and Too Many Sitters	$3.99
❑ MG69205-4	#99	Stacey's Broken Heart	$3.99
❑ MG69206-2	#100	Kristy's Worst Idea	$3.99
❑ MG69207-0	#101	Claudia Kishi, Middle School Dropout	$3.99
❑ MG69208-9	#102	Mary Anne and the Little Princess	$3.99
❑ MG69209-7	#103	Happy Holidays, Jessi	$3.99
❑ MG45575-3		Logan's Story Special Edition Readers' Request	$3.25
❑ MG47118-X		Logan Bruno, Boy Baby-sitter	
		Special Edition Readers' Request	$3.50
❑ MG47756-0		Shannon's Story Special Edition	$3.50
❑ MG47686-6		The Baby-sitters Club Guide to Baby-sitting	$3.25
❑ MG47314-X		The Baby-sitters Club Trivia and Puzzle Fun Book	$2.50
❑ MG48400-1		BSC Portrait Collection: Claudia's Book	$3.50
❑ MG22864-1		BSC Portrait Collection: Dawn's Book	$3.50
❑ MG69181-3		BSC Portrait Collection: Kristy's Book	$3.99
❑ MG22865-X		BSC Portrait Collection: Mary Anne's Book	$3.99
❑ MG48399-4		BSC Portrait Collection: Stacey's Book	$3.50
❑ MG92713-2		The Complete Guide to The Baby-sitters Club	$4.95
❑ MG47151-1		The Baby-sitters Club Chain Letter	$14.95
❑ MG48295-5		The Baby-sitters Club Secret Santa	$14.95
❑ MG45074-3		The Baby-sitters Club Notebook	$2.50
❑ MG44783-1		The Baby-sitters Club Postcard Book	$4.95

Available wherever you buy books...or use this order form.
Scholastic Inc., P.O. Box 7502, 2931 E. McCarty Street, Jefferson City, MO 65102

Please send me the books I have checked above. I am enclosing $_____
(please add $2.00 to cover shipping and handling). Send check or money order–
no cash or C.O.D.s please.

Name_____ Birthdate_____

Address _____

City_____ State/Zip _____

Please allow four to six weeks for delivery. Offer good in the U.S. only. Sorry,
mail orders are not available to residents of Canada. Prices subject to change.

BSC5962

THE BABY-SITTERS CLUB®

by Ann M. Martin

Collect and read these exciting BSC Super Specials, Mysteries, and Super Mysteries along with your favorite Baby-sitters Club books!

BSC Super Specials

❏ BBK44240-6	Baby-sitters on Board! Super Special #1	$3.95
❏ BBK44239-2	Baby-sitters' Summer Vacation Super Special #2	$3.95
❏ BBK43973-1	Baby-sitters' Winter Vacation Super Special #3	$3.95
❏ BBK42493-9	Baby-sitters' Island Adventure Super Special #4	$3.95
❏ BBK43575-2	California Girls! Super Special #5	$3.95
❏ BBK43576-0	New York, New York! Super Special #6	$4.50
❏ BBK44963-X	Snowbound! Super Special #7	$3.95
❏ BBK44962-X	Baby-sitters at Shadow Lake Super Special #8	$3.95
❏ BBK45661-X	Starring The Baby-sitters Club! Super Special #9	$3.95
❏ BBK45674-1	Sea City, Here We Come! Super Special #10	$3.95
❏ BBK47015-9	The Baby-sitters Remember Super Special #11	$3.95
❏ BBK48308-0	Here Come the Bridesmaids! Super Special #12	$3.95
❏ BBK22883-8	Aloha, Baby-sitters! Super Special #13	$4.50

BSC Mysteries

❏ BAI44084-5	#1 Stacey and the Missing Ring	$3.50
❏ BAI44085-3	#2 Beware Dawn!	$3.50
❏ BAI44799-8	#3 Mallory and the Ghost Cat	$3.50
❏ BAI44800-5	#4 Kristy and the Missing Child	$3.50
❏ BAI44801-3	#5 Mary Anne and the Secret in the Attic	$3.50
❏ BAI44961-3	#6 The Mystery at Claudia's House	$3.50
❏ BAI44960-5	#7 Dawn and the Disappearing Dogs	$3.50
❏ BAI44959-1	#8 Jessi and the Jewel Thieves	$3.50
❏ BAI44958-3	#9 Kristy and the Haunted Mansion	$3.50
❏ BAI45696-2	#10 Stacey and the Mystery Money	$3.50

More titles ➡

The Baby-sitters Club books continued...

Available wherever you buy books...or use this order form.

Scholastic Inc., P.O. Box 7502, 2931 East McCarty Street, Jefferson City, MO 65102-7502

Please send me the books I have checked above. I am enclosing $ _____
(please add $2.00 to cover shipping and handling). Send check or money order
— no cash or C.O.D.s please.

Name_____Birthdate_____

Address _____

City_____State/Zip_____

Please allow four to six weeks for delivery. Offer good in the U.S. only. Sorry, mail orders are not available to residents of Canada. Prices subject to change.

BSCM496

The New THE BABY-SITTERS CLUB® FAN CLUB

Only $8.95!
Plus $2.00 Postage and Handling

Sign up now for a year of great friendships and terrific memories!

★ **110-mm camera!**
Take photos of your pals!

★ **Mini-photo album**
Fill it with your best pics!

★ **Diary (with lock!)**
For your favorite memories...and secret thoughts!

★ **Stationery note cards and stickers**
Send letters to your far-away friends!

★ **Eight cool pencils**
With the signatures of different baby-sitters!

★ **Full-color BSC poster**

★ **Subscription to the official BSC newsletter***

★ **Special keepsake shipper**

Amazing stuff!

PHOTOS

To get your fan club pack (in the U.S. and Canada only), just fill out the coupon or write the information on a 3" x 5" card and send it to us with your check or money order. U.S. residents: $8.95 plus $2.00 postage and handling to The New BSC FAN CLUB, Scholastic Inc. P.O. Box 7500, 2931 East McCarty Street, Jefferson City, MO 65102. Canadian residents: $13.95 plus $2.00 postage and handling to The New BSC FAN CLUB, Scholastic Canada, 123 Newkirk Road, Richmond Hill, Ontario, L4C3G5. Offer expires 9/30/97. Offer good for one year from date of receipt. Please allow 4-6 weeks for your introductory pack to arrive.

*First newsletter is sent after introductory pack. You will receive at least 4 newsletters during your one-year membership.

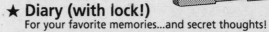

Hurry! Send me my New Baby-sitters Club Fan Club Pack. I am enclosing my check or money order (no cash please) for U.S. residents: $10.95 ($8.95 plus $2.00) and for Canadian residents: $15.95 ($13.95 plus $2.00).

Name_____ Birthdate_____
      First   Last   D / M / Y

Address_____

City_____ State_____ Zip_____

Telephone (   )_____ Boy_____ Girl_____

Where did you buy this book? ❑ Bookstore ❑ Book Fair ❑ Book Club ❑ Other_____

■SCHOLASTIC

BABB397